LITTLE
BIRD
LANDS

LITTLE BIRD LANDS

KAREN McCOMBIE

nosy crow

First published in the UK in 2020 by Nosy Crow Ltd
The Crow's Nest, 14 Baden Place
Crosby Row, London, SE1 1YW

Nosy Crow and associated logos are trademarks and/or registered
trademarks of Nosy Crow Ltd

A CIP catalogue record for this book is available from the
British Library.

Printed and bound in Great Britain by Clays Ltd, Elcograf S.p.A.
Typeset by Tiger Media

Papers used by Nosy Crow are made from wood grown in
sustainable forests

ISBN: 978 1 78800 533 3

www.nosycrow.com

FOR
JEANNIE McCOMBIE,
WHO DREAMED OF MORE...
KMcC

"IS BRÀITHREAN SINN UILE,
FAIR DHÒMHSA DO LÀMH..."

"COME GIVE ME YOUR HAND,
WE ARE 'FAMILY', ALL OF US..."

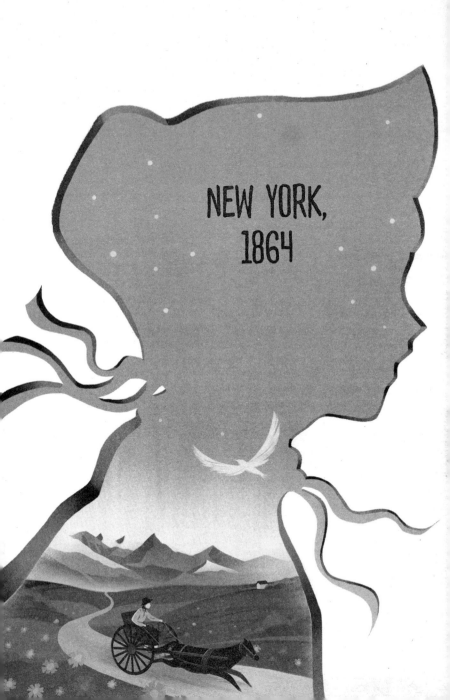

NEW YORK,
1864

CHAPTER 1

Fifteen years ago, my mother looked down upon me – cradled and broken in her arms – and made a wish. She wished that I might live, since it seemed likely that I would not.

But I was a determined little thing; determined *not* to die. And thanks to my mother's words of strength and courage, whispered in her beloved Scots Gaelic language, I thrived.

Hopeful and heartened, Mother dared to make a *second* wish.

She wished that I might live a long and peaceful life, never leaving the small Scottish island that was home to our family. That wish did *not* come true … and I for one am glad of it. For if I had stayed on Tornish all my days, I would never have known an evening like tonight!

How my heart soared to see the glow of the distant lights of New York City as we left Mrs Drummond's farmhouse – where we lodge – and rollicked along dark country lanes till the cartwheels met the smoothness of the new-built roads.

And the very racket of the city! Songs of street musicians, roars of peddlers, the hiss of the hundreds of gaslights illuminating grand carriages, gawping families and drunken carousers stumbling from saloons…

Then to be lost in a cloud of words I did not understand as we stood in the queue for the world-famous Barnum's American Museum. Folk about us talked excitedly in a tumult of different tongues, of the wonders they'd see inside I supposed. Scientific exhibits, curiosities from around the globe, strange creatures never before seen.

And of course, if I had stayed in Tornish, I would never, *never* have found myself face-to-face with a monster…

"What *is* it, Little Bird?" Marthy-Jane asks me, teetering on tiptoe on the wooden viewing platform, her eyes just level with the glass window. Her small hand clutches my weaker one, nails as fine as pale pink seashells pinching my skin.

She gazes up at me for an answer. When I am not helping her grandmother around the farmyard, or with the laundry she takes in for the rich of the city, I help Marthy-Jane Drummond practise her letters and numbers. But right now I am too taken aback to act like a teacher and give her an explanation; I can do nothing but shake my head stupidly. For when the great, white, waxy bulk of a monster floats in front of you – one of its glossy, dark, apple-sized eyes locked on to yours – it is difficult to be certain of anything, to find a tongue in your head even.

"It is a bel ... a bel ... *something* whale," I hear Lachlan saying as he tries to read the sign by the huge tank, while folk jostle alongside us for a good spot to see the creature.

Mind you, my eleven-year-old brother would struggle to read the brass plaque even if he were quite alone in front of it. He can speak and chatter as quickly as the mynah bird in Mrs Drummond's parlour, but when it comes to reading and writing he stumbles as if words were rocks and ditches along a path, set on tripping him up. His teacher despairs of him.

"A *beluga* whale." Father's more certain voice comes from behind us. "It was captured off the coast of Labrador, with great difficulty, it says, and transported here."

As I listen to Father read from the plaque, I suddenly think *not* of the animal's capture or the means used to bring it to New York, but of how on earth they got the thing up the stairs of this building, all the way to the second floor!

"Dear me; Labrador is up in Canada. This beast has come from the great seas there only to be stuck in a tank," I hear Mrs Drummond add with a sorrowful sigh. "Poor thing…"

I suppose our landlady will still be gripping Father's arm. She is not in the best of spirits, and I think regrets letting herself be persuaded to come to the yearly Evacuation Day celebrations. She is used to the quiet life of her farm, she always says, though it gets less quiet every day. There is the building of Central Park nearby – where Father works as a stonemason – and the never-ending clunk, hammer and boom of explosions as the new roads and buildings march closer to small farms like Mrs Drummond's, ready to swallow them up whole.

"It's worse than that *last* one we looked at," I hear her grumble, in a voice that makes her own Scottish heritage quite clear, though *she* last saw the shores of her homeland more than half-a-century ago, while my *own* little family have been here but two years.

Mrs Drummond's grumbling is on account of her not caring for the "Happy Family" exhibit we just saw on the fifth floor. It is a large menagerie which Mr P. T. Barnum himself had seen on a trip to Scotland – of all places! – and shipped back to New York to add to his own renowned collections. Inside the large cage are cats and rats, rabbits and foxes, animals that would normally hunt and set upon each other in the wild, but here live contentedly together. "Unnatural…" Mrs Drummond said sourly of it.

And now, as I stand eye-to-eye with this colossus, I suddenly feel as agitated as Mrs Drummond. How trapped must the whale feel? Does it look at all our faces pressed to the glass and wish itself far away, in the pure, measureless ocean it was plucked from?

"Can we go, please?" I say, turning quickly to Father and Mrs Drummond, not wishing to gaze upon the whale in its watery prison a moment longer.

"Of, course," says Father, reaching out to lift Marthy-Jane into his arms, the way he'd so easily lift my brother and myself – both our older sisters too – once upon a time. "What would you like to see next?"

"The waxworks, please, Father!" says Lachlan, without hesitation. "There's one of the famous Siamese twins Eng and Chang – they are joined at the stomach! And there is also one of General Tom Thumb who is a grown man but stands *smaller* than Marthy-Jane! Oh, and after the waxworks we *have* to see the living bearded lady, and—"

"Robert, did you say there was a lecture hall in here, where we may sit awhile?" Mrs Drummond asks Father. She dotes on him, as she does all of us. I think we are as good as family to her, what with her only son – Marthy-Jane's father – away at war in the Union Army, and Marthy-Jane's mother dead from tuberculosis, that cruel disease that snuffed out my *own* mother's life.

"Yes, and a talk might be starting there soon," says Father, jostling a path for us through the crowds and ignoring Lachlan's disappointed sigh.

A few minutes later we find ourselves outside the lecture hall, waiting for the doors to be opened and the talk to commence. Lachlan stands a little away from us, leaning at the window and taking in the hustle and bustle below while he eats the sugared-coconut shavings that he bought from a Chinese street vendor on the way here. My brother is very taken with Manhattan, the very beating heart of New York, and is determined to be a bellboy in a grand hotel one day. Either that or a soldier in the army, if the war is still raging when he is of an age to serve. (*Please* let the war be over before that time!)

"Listen to this," says Father, reading from a pamphlet he has been handed. "We are about to see Miss Annie Swan, who stands at *eight feet* in height, and is to discuss giants throughout history! Ah, she is from Nova Scotia, in Canada, Mrs Drummond. Wasn't that where your *own* family first settled when they came to this continent?"

"Indeed, yes!" says Mrs Drummond, and she and Father begin to talk, as they so often do, about where the Scots emigrated to and from over the years.

"Little Bird?" says Marthy-Jane, tugging at my hand. I am always gladdened to hear her call me by my old pet name; no one has had any use for it since we left Tornish. To everyone but Marthy-Jane I am plain Bridie these days. Mostly, being Bridie is just fine, but sometimes I do miss the Little Bird I once was.

"What is it, *m'eudail?*" I ask, calling her "my treasure" in the Gaelic words I grew up with.

She is only a little thing and is perhaps weary of waiting. She'll surely be wanting to hear one of my stories to pass the time ... stories of my childhood on the island, then of my family's life in the grand Scottish city of Glasgow, and of our stomach-churning journey across the sea to New York. She thrills to the tales of the mischief-making my old friend Will and I got up to back on Tornish, and of the ways I drove my bossy sisters Ishbel and Effie to distraction. She's fond too of hearing about the well-to-do visitors who came to the island and became our friends: Samuel the portrait painter and Caroline, the young lady who arrived shrouded in black mourning clothes. Most of all she loves hearing about Patch, the wee terrier we sadly had to leave behind in Scotland.

I only tell her the cheerful stories, of course. I wouldn't want to scare her with *all* of the truth, of the fear we sometimes lived with and the risky decisions my family had to make...

"Can I tell you something?" she says in reply, looking

upon me with such a serious expression for one so young.

"Of course," I say, crouching down to show that I am listening keenly to whatever troubles her.

"You are very small and pretty, like a doll," she whispers, her blue eyes wide, her free hand stroking my long black hair, as if I am a beloved cat she cares for.

"Well, that is very kind of you to say," I reply, smiling at her peculiar compliment.

I *am* small and slight for my age; even Lachlan, four years my junior, is taller than me. But I have never thought of myself as delicate and doll-like.

"And I think that you should *not* be here," Marthy-Jane whispers again, this time more urgently.

"Why do you think that?" I ask, trying not to laugh at her earnestness, yet puzzling at her meaning.

"What if Mr Barnum should appear? What if he sees your ... differences?" As she speaks, Marthy-Jane nods at the hand that I have placed on her arm, then glances down in the direction of my polished leather boots. "What if he wants to steal you away for his museum?"

Ah, now I understand. She talks of the weakness in my left hand and the twisting of my left foot.

"Oh, I'm not enough of an oddity for this museum, I'm sure!" I tell my little friend.

While I may be certain that the mighty Mr Barnum would not consider me suitable enough to be one of his human exhibits – to be goggled at and mimicked and pitied – I am suddenly very glad for the soft, laced boot that hides my foot, and the sleeves of the too-large second-hand winter jacket that half covers my withered hand.

I am also aware of an uncomfortable restlessness stirring inside me, and I suddenly wish that we could all leave this curious place and—

"Bridie! Father!" Lachlan calls to us, his voice loud so that he can be heard above some shouting – some merry-making? – going on outside in the street. "There is smoke coming from the hotel over the way, and people are running from the entrance!"

"What's that, Lachlan?" asks Father, striding swiftly towards my brother before I can get up off my knees.

"FIRE! FIRE!"

Along with every person waiting outside the lecture hall, my head turns in the direction of the stairs from where this cry has come. For the merest moment, I think it must be someone who, like Lachlan, has spied the disturbance in the building nearby.

But then I see the haze of smoke at the end of the long, tiled corridor, and a strange chemical stench catches, *scratches* at my throat.

"FIRE! RUN! FIRE!" call out more voices, and I am on my feet, gripping tight to Marthy-Jane as I look to Father.

"Go!" he calls out to me as he ushers Lachlan and Mrs Drummond ahead of him.

And now Marthy-Jane and I are in a crush of folk, streaming away from the smoke to what we must all hope is another exit in this fog of panic. And sure enough, here is the wide, sweeping stairwell, and we are quickly upon it, a thunder of feet and a shudder of panting breaths as we hurry in a human stream downwards.

There is a soft and steady surge of bodies pushing around us, and I cannot make out where Father, Lachlan and Mrs Drummond are, but still I hold tight to Marthy-Jane *and* remain calm – until a series of screams ring out. The surge becomes an unsettling, unsteadying jostle, and I turn my head sharply, expecting to spy flames licking at the walls of the floor above.

Instead I am instantly aware of the cause of the screaming; a desperately worried woman is in our midst. A desperately worried woman who towers above us, her great height alarming these already frightened people.

The crush on the stairs; it suddenly becomes the forceful surge of a wave that might well tip us forward. And in that sliver of a panicked second, I clearly picture three beloved faces. In my mind's eye I see the smile of my childhood friend Will, who probably thinks I am settled still in Glasgow, since that was where my

11

family were bound when we fled Tornish. I see my older sisters Ishbel and Effie, who chose *not* to come with Father, Lachlan and me to America.

Will, Ishbel and Effie.

All three lost from me; I have heard nothing from them and have no idea what has become of them.

And for their part, they have no idea that *I* might be about to die here in New York, in this strange museum, in a stampede, in a fire, by the side of Miss Annie Swan, the tallest woman in the world.

But wait... I have come close to death and danger since the day I was born – am I not as determined as I have ever been to survive?

"Hold tight. We'll be fine!" I assure Marthy-Jane as I picture my mother just outside the now-wide open doors to the street, waving a corner of her knitted shawl like a flag, guiding us onward...

COPPER COUNTRY,
MICHIGAN

CHAPTER 2

Clusters of iron-grey clouds bluster and bump me this way and that.

The wind twists my skirt tight about my legs then puffs it out again.

I flap and fly back and forth, knowing I have not the strength for the whole journey across the ocean.

"I don't know where I am … but Father says it is for the best!" I call out, hoping that a faint trace of my voice will carry on the eastern wind, so it can trail my words all the way across the great, wide Atlantic, till the speckles of islands that cling to the west coast of Scotland come into view.

Then the wind will finally spy Tornish, and whirl my words to the ground like loose feathers, easing so that they gently drop on to Mother's grave in the quiet, peaceful churchyard there…

"Bridie! Bridie, wake up!"

My brother shakes me hard, and my uneasy dream drifts away like damp fog.

LITTLE BIRD LANDS

"We're nearly there!" Lachlan says excitedly. His sadness at leaving New York and the future he saw for himself in the city has been tempered with a boyish thrill of the new.

When we first arrived in America two years ago, our heads and hearts were full of plans to travel west, to find ourselves a little piece of wilderness to farm in a place of rippling prairies and blue skies wide as the sea. But we are not in the west. For the "nearly there" my brother speaks of is the densely wooded, northernmost tip of Michigan, which itself is one of the most northerly states of the United States of America.

War was the reason that Father abandoned our plans to homestead when we first landed at the emigration depot in New York back in '62. We had the misfortune to come to a country that was – and still is – fighting a terrible battle with itself. The northern, Union states fight southern, Confederate states. Those that want all the states of this vast country to stay together, those states that want to break away. Those *against* slavery, those very much *for* this unthinkable practice. So in those early days, Father lost his nerve – he thought it wise to stay near New York, far from the fighting and battlegrounds.

Only the fighting came to *us*, didn't it? One week ago, on the night of the Evacuation Day celebrations, Confederate supporters slunk around the city, leaving carefully crafted firebombs in hotels, theatres, and of course at Barnum's American Museum…

"Hurry! You can see Hawk's Point!" says Lachlan, holding out his hand to me.

"Thank you," I reply as I take hold of it and stamp my boots on the deck to bring life back to my frozen feet.

But standing up so fast was foolish. Maddeningly, I am as feeble as one of the newborn kittens Marthy-Jane and I used to play with back in Mrs Drummond's barn. Oh, I cannot bear to feel this poorly! It seems so unfair that I was strong enough to escape the museum with Marthy-Jane and yet the chemicals used to set the fire – poisonous packages of sulphur, naptha and quicklime – have weakened my chest and let some infection in.

Still, I must do my best; not only to appear well and cheerful for Father's sake and Lachlan's, but for myself. If we are to have a new start here, I must set aside what I'd have *hoped* for and settle for what I *have* – an adventure!

And today, this hour, the adventure begins with forested cliffs rising dizzingly high to the left as we come close to shore. The prow of the steamship snaps and crunches through the thin crust of ice on the surface of the huge lake we're crossing. Lachlan leads me to the railing nearby so I can better see the view of the town itself … and through fluttering flecks of snow, I see the raggedy wooden and tar-papered rooftops of Hawk's Point; a half-built mining town teetering on the edge of Lake Superior, in the shadow of those tree-peppered cliffs. A remote place of Chippewa Indians, French-Canadian trappers, fur traders and wild nature – and of miners too, more recently, digging deep underground for copper, wanted the world over for decoration, pots and pans, industry and building. And this precious, rose-gold metal is the reason the coastline here is dotted with big, bustling mining towns and new, smaller settlements like the one we are headed for.

How beautiful will copper be in the raw? Will the very streets gleam and twinkle with pebbles of it, I wonder?

"Where is Father?" I now think to ask Lachlan, trying to steady myself with a deep breath – though all that does is make me cough.

"He went to ask someone how long it'll take till we dock," says Lachlan, too taken with the view to notice the coughing that now wracks and ruins me.

My brother has become so used to my constant coughing this last week that I think he barely notices it now. As for Father, I see him always watch me. I know he wished I were better than I have been for the days of travelling we have undertaken, but after the attack he did not want to stay in New York a minute longer. So I remember our juddering train journey to Buffalo, the steamship voyages across three of the Great Lakes in the north – Eerie, Huron and finally Superior – through a hot, murky haze of fever and exhaustion.

"Oh!" I call out, as the boat lurches and loses me my balance.

I reach out for Lachlan's arm, but my younger brother has quite forgotten he has a sickly sister; in his excitement at seeing the shanty town and harbour growing ever closer, he has hurried back to rejoin the throng of folk who stand at the front of the ship, bundled in layers of coats and scarves and shawls against the slap of the winter winds and the lightly drifting snow.

And then a strong arm comes about me, and I feel moored again.

"Are you all right, Bridie?" says Father, gazing into my face in concern. His scruffy dark-red hair and beard bring a cheer of colour against the bruised sky and whirling snowflakes.

"I'm fine," I lie, wishing – despite my best intentions to be cheerful – that I was resting in my bed in our rooms at Mrs Drummond's, with the chicken coop and its chirping inhabitants outside the window and the merry sound of our landlady clattering about in the kitchen downstairs. I hold still for a second and can almost hear her singing "The Bonnie Banks of Loch Lomond" or some other Scottish song that Marthy-Jane likes to skip and dance around to.

"I'm not sure you *are* quite fine yet, Bridie, but once we're settled you'll be back to your usual good health," Father says with a nod, then stands straight and looks about him. "Ah, now … do you hear that?"

"Do you mean the ice cracking?" I ask.

"No. Listen again!"

Ah, now I do hear something else. I hear a hard, metallic thumping and presume it to be a mechanical matter from the bowels of the ship as it slows and gets ready to dock. I nod in reply, though it makes my head swirl unpleasantly.

"*That* is the sound of a stamp mill," Father says.

"A stamp mill?" I repeat questioningly.

"Look. Can you see the top of that tall wooden structure just rising above the roofs of those buildings?" he asks.

"The thing that looks like a capital 'H'?" I check.

"Yes! Though we can't make it out from here, between the wooden struts are great metal hammers that come down one after the other upon rocks to crush them, and so release the copper welded inside."

"How do you know about that, Father?" I ask, peering in the direction of the noisy piece of mining machinery.

"Gordon described it to me," Father says, his face quite lit up with the marvel of it all.

Gordon. I never met this Gordon Gillespie, another

Highlander who Father worked alongside in the making of Central Park. If it were not for him and his brother – who needed a winter tenant for his carpentry store in Hawk's Point – we would not have found ourselves here.

"What luck to have found this place." Father sighs contentedly, before looking at me with a knowing smile. "Or is it the 'invisible thread', Bridie?"

"Aye, Father, I suppose it is," I say, remembering the conversation we once had around the table at Mrs Drummond's.

We'd been speaking of the peculiar luck or coincidence that meant newly arrived immigrants to America – whether they be from Scotland, Russia, China or whichever land – should end up travelling hundreds or sometimes *thousands* of miles to some particular settlement, only to find themselves living right next to a neighbour from their old village back home!

But of course it is not luck or coincidence at all. For an immigrant coming to a new land, there is sense and comfort in following the routes and trails of those who have gone before. That night I told the others that I likened this to an invisible thread – fine as a spider's web – that stretched almost magically from people's homelands, across the ocean, only to weave and wander its way all across this vast country.

And so our invisible thread has brought us here...

"Father, Bridie – listen!" Lachlan calls out to us over his shoulder.

At first I suppose that Lachlan is talking of the stamp mill's steady chest-pounding clatter and bang, but there is another sound above it – the pleasing peal of a bell and sharp trill of whistling.

"The townsfolk are glad for us to be coming, Father!" Lachlan calls out again in delight.

"It seems so." Father laughs at my brother's words, before turning to me. "Is that not a good omen, Bridie? Showing us that we are in the right place? That we three shall be content here?"

My sister Effie was always one for omens, but I don't truthfully think my city-loving sister would see any good ones here, in this tucked-away corner of a faraway state, in this biting cold.

"I hope so, Father!" I say as brightly as I can, feeling my chest burn and tighten after my last coughing fit.

But Father is now busy calling for my brother and hurriedly sorting through our luggage. In a few short minutes we are all laden like packhorses with bags and satchels, while Father and Lachlan carry the heavy trunk between them.

"Are the people of Hawk's Point always as friendly and welcoming?" Father asks the deckhand who is wrestling with the gangplank that will let us ashore.

"They are not welcoming *you*, sir," the deckhand replies in some burred, Scandinavian accent. "They welcome the ship and the goods it brings."

I see Father's smile fade a little; so much for the good omen he foresaw.

"They all know that this is the last sailing of the year," the deckhand continues. "Nothing more's coming though this way till spring."

At that last remark, I see Father's smile reignite, while *I* cannot help myself shivering a little at the notion that we are to be stranded for months in this unknown place, as trapped as Mr P. T. Barnum's beluga whale in its watery jail. However, Father clearly feels that we are all safely marooned, so very far from the Civil War and its battles — and acts of terror done in its name.

But if we are to be cut off from the world here, who will be our neighbours? I gaze out at the faces in the throng and see some women, perhaps twenty or so children of all ages, several babes-in-arms, and many rough-looking men in battered clothing, some with white clay pipes wedged in their mouths. Miners, they'll be, taking time away from their underground burrowing to collect provisions for the coming winter.

"*Thoir an aire,* Bridie!"

Father tells me to take care in Gaelic as the crowd of locals jostle close to the end of the gangplank, leaving little space for us to disembark.

LITTLE BIRD LANDS

And the single-minded business and chatter of the crowd carries on as we finally step on to dry land and seek out a cart that might take our luggage and chest to our new lodgings, at the carpenter's store. A handcart is secured, and its owner is a young Indian man, I'm surprised to see. I have not met such a person before. New York's streets team with people from countries far and wide across Europe and Asia, but if an Indian has walked the city's streets, I have not been lucky enough to see one. I sneak a sideways glance at him, at his still, high-cheeked face, his long, black, braided hair and loose suede trousers, which he wears alongside a black jacket, shirt, waistcoat and wide-rimmed felt hat. His belt is unusual, though – it is a band made of many small, coloured beads.

As we walk towards what looks like one single street of shanty buildings, I try to catch a glimpse of the belt again, to make out the intricate pattern of it. But then I hear a raised voice and glance back towards the bustle of the harbour-front.

"You cannot be!" a very smartly dressed man is yelling, his face as florid red as his hair is startlingly white-blond. He is yelling at a tall woman who must have come from the ship, guessing from the luggage piled at her feet.

"Well, as you can clearly see, I am," the bespectacled woman answers calmly, hands stuffed in the deep pockets of her long, thick overcoat.

"I'm expecting a STEPHEN Spicer," the man bellows.

"You have STEPHANIE Spicer, I'm afraid, so we'll just have to make the best of it, won't we?" the woman states flatly.

"Bridie!"

I turn in the direction of my brother's call and see that a skinny, rough-haired dog – with extraordinarily pale-grey eyes – seems to be padding alongside Lachlan, Father and the rattling cart and its owner. They are all swiftly leaving me dawdling, and so I do my best to make my leaden legs follow after them.

The conversation between the woman and the smartly dressed man – I can no longer hear it. But I suspect I'll find out what it's all about soon enough. In a place this small there can be no secrets, can there?

Then again, I wish most sincerely that no one will find out *ours*... Young Lachlan MacKerrie, a black-hearted thief. Our father Robert MacKerrie, suspected of a murder plot. And myself, Bridie MacKerrie, a kidnapper would you believe.

No, some secrets need to stay buried where they belong, back in Scotland...

CHAPTER 3

"It's a fine-looking animal!" says Father, his boots slip-sliding on the frozen ruts of the road.

The Indian nods in agreement as he pulls the handcart between two rows of low, roughly built wooden buildings.

In truth, the grey-eyed dog looks like some wild creature. A wolf from the mountains. But it walks – in its springy way – quite peaceably at the side of its master.

"What kind of dog is it, sir?" Lachlan asks.

The young man gives my brother a startled smile. Perhaps he is not used to being addressed as "sir". "He's an Alaskan husky. Got him as a pup from a hunter fella in a town along the coast. Alaskan huskies are working dogs up in Canada and further north."

"Has he got a name?" asks Lachlan.

"I call him Odayan," the man answers with a shrug, and the dog looks up sharply at him.

"Odayan... Odayan..." Lachlan carefully repeats,

earning a glance from the dog himself. "Is that an Indian name?"

"Yes."

"What does it mean?" Lachlan persists, hop-skipping alongside the dog and risking a shy stroke of its head. The wary dog lowers itself away from my brother's hand.

"Dog," says the Indian, with a hint of a smile.

"Dog!" Lachlan laughs, trying a second stroke, which this time the creature does not shy away from, only giving an unsure shiver.

But Lachlan's laugh has a crack to it, and sure enough, while my brother's mouth smiles, I see him quickly wiping at his eyes with the sleeve of his thick jacket.

The Indian notices; he frowns.

"We had a dog back in Scotland," I tell the man, blinking as snowflakes land on my lashes. "We were not able to bring it when we came to America."

Lachlan will sometimes talk fondly and sadly of the little terrier Patch, though he will not mention our older sisters any more. Perhaps it's because Father told us both that it might be better not to speak of them, as it is too hard on the heart. I understand what Father means, but I don't know if I think the same way. There are times when I would love nothing better than to reminisce about how much my older sisters maddened me with their nagging and nit-picking, and yet how much I loved them. As for Lachlan, it seems he finds it easier to mourn the loss of Patch than the loss of Ishbel and Effie. Or perhaps it is his way of secretly mourning all three?

A sudden, sharp whistle catches my attention, and that of the others. The dog gives a low, menacing growl, but quickly quietens with a warning hiss from its owner.

The whistler is a boy, somewhere between Lachlan's age and mine. He watches as we approach the wooden building he leans against. A worn cap is set back on his fair-haired head, and there's a cocky smile on his face. The building behind him is one-storey high, the same as all the others — most still part-built — up and down the short stretch of street. It is a simple style; two glass windows on either side of a door of planks, and a badly hand-painted sign above it that reads "Nat's Store". It is a very long way from the grand, gas-lit streets and avenues of New York, and even the Glasgow I knew before it...

But Lachlan isn't much interested in the boy. Drying his nose on his jacket sleeve, he stares at the man and his dog, impressed, I think, by how obedient the husky is.

"Are you an *actual* Indian, sir?" he finally plucks up the courage to ask.

"He's a Chippewa injun. Ain't you, Jean?" the boy calls over, saying the man's name in the French way rather than the Scottish.

"I am *Anishinaabe*," the Indian answers almost under his breath.

I don't know if that means he's correcting the boy's telling of his tribe name or if it is his real name...

"Does your whole tribe live here?" Lachlan asks Jean, glancing around hopefully.

"Nah, most of 'em got moved on years ago," the boy calls out again, punctuating his words with a spit on the ground. "Live on the reservation miles from here, don't they, Jean?"

Reservations; I've read of those in Father's newspapers. The US government paid money to many Indian tribes for their land, moving them on to other areas – "reservations". I did not think it would happen here, in this great, quiet state. I thought there'd be *more* than enough room for all types of folk to live their lives.

"Then there's injuns like Jean," the boy continues, "who like to hang around the white settlements, trying to earn a buck from us."

I can hardly believe that someone who is just a scruffy boy can dare to speak to a grown man with such cheek!

The Indian blanks the boy. Instead, he looks to Father and says, "This is the place," while nodding towards Nat's Store.

"It's MY place too – I'm Charlie Nathaniel and my father is Nat!" the boy bellows, pointing up at the sign.

Ah, so the fact that his father is a storekeeper makes this lad feel he is "better" than the young man. How it vexes me when folk see themselves as more powerful than others! The Tornish islanders had to be meek and mild in front of the landowning Laird, as well as his dreadful snob of a wife and spoilt, spiteful daughter, Miss Kitty. I *had* hoped it would not be this way in America, that folk would be more equal, as I hear President Abraham Lincoln himself has said, and presidents before him whose names I do not know. It seems that it is not the case, sadly.

"Well, thank you for your help," Father says, holding out his hand to shake the Indian's. "I should have introduced myself earlier. I'm Robert MacKerrie, and these are my children Bridie and Lachlan."

The Indian seems surprised at the polite introduction, but sets the barrow down so he has a hand free to shake Father's in return.

"I'm Jean Paquette," he says. "I have a place in the woods, but I'm around if you ever need help with anything. I can turn my hand to fixing most things."

"I'll certainly bear that in mind, Jean," says Father, taking leave of the handshake so that he can find some coins in his jacket pocket to pay the Indian.

"So we are to live *here*?" asks Lachlan, his eyes roving over the store-front we stopped in front of. He now looks warily at the cocky boy, I notice.

"No – I was told that the gentleman who owns this place holds the keys to the building *we'll* be looking after," says Father.

The Indian snorts as he drops his coins into a small pouch that's as finely beaded as the belt around his waist. The snort was on account of the word "gentleman", I think.

"Is this where I can buy supplies too?" Father asks of the Indian, since he still has our luggage on his handcart.

"It's the *only* place to buy *anything*, and Nat will be very pleased to take all your money from you in any way he can," says the Indian. "It's the only general store in Hawk's Point, and it's the post office and saloon too, on Saturday night, after the miners have been paid…"

My heart surges with hope when I hear the words "post office". I sent two letters – one to Ishbel and one to Effie – before we left New York, telling them where we were headed. They'll probably go unanswered, as all the others have, but I cannot help wishing for a miracle, for a reply. Though even if that miracle *did* happen, there'll be no ship and so no postal deliveries for many months, till the sunshine of spring melts the ice on Lake Superior.

"I'll take your bags over to Gillespie's place," adds the Indian, moving off across the street, all the while glowering at the storekeeper's son.

The boy just grins, then kicks the door open for us in

a brutish kind of welcome. Following him inside, we find ourselves in the gloom of a low-lit room. There is a counter in front of us, but it is hard to see with the boxes and sacks piled up around it and against it and on top of it. Behind are shelves laden with shapes I can't quite make out as my eyes adjust to the lack of brightness. The large bulk of a saddle is easily recognisable on the floor to my left, though, while a simple long bench runs along the right-hand wall.

"Pa!" the boy hollers.

"What?" a gruff voice calls out from a doorway just behind the counter.

"You got customers!" says the boy, sliding around to the opposite side of the counter to us, just as a large, unkempt man comes ambling out from some unseen back room.

The man seems in an ill humour, like a bear woken from its winter sleep. And he also looks as if he may have had some trouble with a bear or some such dangerous creature; he has much scarring across his upper face, the skin puckered and one eye quite gone, the emptiness of it sewn shut.

"Are you Mr Nathaniel?" Father asks him.

"I am. And who might you be?" the man answers warily in a muddled accent that is for the most part Yankee.

"My name is Robert MacKerrie," Father explains.

"I am here to tenant the building of a carpenter called Gillespie?"

The man looks a little taken aback, and studies Father for a second.

"Wasn't that the place you're planning on renting out for lodgings, Pa?" the boy asks, earning himself a sharp clip around the ear.

"Ow!"

I quickly exchange a shocked look with Lachlan.

"It got so late in the season, I didn't think Gillespie had found anyone," says this Mr Nathaniel, rummaging for something under his counter. "Here, for the padlock and chain on the door – catch."

A chunky key, attached with twine to a small piece of wood, is hurled in Father's direction.

"Er … *tapadh leibh*…" Father thanks him, speaking in Gaelic in the surprise of the moment.

The man pauses, frowns, then says, *"Cò as a thàinig sibh?"*

A smile breaks over Father's face when he hears the storekeeper speak in his own tongue, asking where we have come from. Father no doubt sees the glimmer of the invisible thread again, and will think it *another* good omen for us.

"We're from the Highlands … from the island of Tornish," Father replies to the question.

"Tornish? Never heard of it," the man says with a disinterested shrug.

"Ah, it's a small place, I suppose," Father carries on regardless, hiding his disappointment with a broad smile. "Though we have been in Glasgow and then New York of late. Mr Gillespie sent word to his brother in New York that he was looking for a reliable person to look after his place before he comes back in spring..."

Mr Nathaniel does not answer, does not listen I suspect. For he is now too busy sneering at a girl I had not noticed before. She comes quietly out of the shadows, cradling a bundle of candles. Her skin is a rich brown, her hair black like mine but tied into two short, thick braids while my own hangs loose and messy down my back, escaping as it always does from tying.

"And where is it you're from?" Father asks the storekeeper, trying to gain his attention once more.

"From Wisconsin – but my mother was Scottish, from Inverness. She taught me some Gaelic," he answers in a bored voice, his gaze on the girl's hand as it reaches out to him, coins nestled in the soft pink of her palm.

Like a striking snake, Mr Nathaniel grabs the girl by her wrist. I watch in shock as he twists it sharply to the right, causing the coins to spill on the counter. Then he lets go, and with an equally sharp push of her hand, he nods at the door.

"Off you go!" he bellows in English, when she does not move.

I feel Lachlan do something he never does any more;

he reaches for my hand.

"Sir, I'm expected to bring home change…" the girl says softly.

"Are you now," says the scarred man. "Pity there's none coming."

"But my master will—"

"GO!"

With her head bowed, the girl pulls her shawl about her and hurries away, the heavy door of the store creaking behind her.

Father, so very happy a moment ago, stands with his mouth hanging a little open, startled that the storekeeper has treated this girl so harshly. The good omen he hoped for? It was not to be, it seems.

But before he can think what to say, Mr Nathaniel turns to me.

"And what are you staring at, missy? My face frightens you, does it?" he asks.

He is quite the fool if he thinks it is his *face* rather than his manner that have caused me to glower at him. And he has accused quite the wrong person of judging a scar or some other difference.

"Now, now," I hear Father say in the soft but firm voice he would use back on Tornish, as an elder who would seek to soften hardened feelings between neighbours with a grudge against each other.

But I do not need or heed Father's gentle words. My

hackles are risen like that dog's outside when he set eyes on Mr Nathaniel's son.

"Why would your face frighten me, sir?" I say as boldly as I can, letting go of Lachlan's hand so that I can rest both of mine on the counter. Now the storekeeper can see quite clearly that I have differences of my own. And in that moment, I think of our family friend Caroline back in Scotland – the woman hidden under black mourning clothes – who was scarred with burns from a house fire and yet was one of the kindest, most beautiful people I have ever met.

"Urgh…" comes a small sound of disgust from the storekeeper's son as he gazes upon my weaker, withered hand. I think I would expect nothing less of him and do not bother to look his way. It is the storekeeper himself who I dare to glare at.

I watch him glance down at my mismatching hands resting on the counter, but the sight of them does not seem to soften him. Instead he lifts his eyes to Father and says, "Quite the little vixen, isn't she?"

Father's face darkens, but any words he plans to say are interrupted by the door being flung open.

"Mr Nathaniel!" calls out the smartly dressed man with the shock of white-blond hair that I saw back at the harbourside. "We have a problem."

"And what might that be, Mr Eriksson? Did the new doctor not arrive?" asks the storekeeper, folding his arms across the waistcoat that struggles to stretch over his rounded stomach. "I told you you'd be hard-pressed to find anyone to take the job. You might be the mine manager but you're no miracle worker…"

"Thank you, but I *have* arrived, and I *have* taken the job, with no miracle required," a voice says, and into the store strides the tall woman from the ship, shaking snow from the shoulders of her very mannish-looking coat. "My name is Dr Stephanie Spicer."

I think it's fair to say that everyone's jaw has dropped, except for this Mr Eriksson, who is clenching his own jaws so tightly I worry it'll be a *dentist* he'll need next.

"*Is* there such a thing as a woman doctor?" Lachlan asks in wonder.

"There are certainly a few of us. I trained at the Female Medical College of Pennsylvania," the woman replies smartly. "I have just shown Mr Eriksson my certificate of qualification. Would you like to see it too, young man?"

"Um … no," Lachlan says shyly, shuffling closer to me.

"A *woman* doctor?" Mr Nathaniel grumbles, as if he can't quite believe what his one good eye is seeing. "No, no, no. As if this place can get any more damned…"

"Damned!" Charlie gleefully repeats the swearword.

Another swift clip around the head shushes the boy once more.

"Ow! But *you* said it first!"

"Shut up – or I've got another one of those for ya!" the storekeeper orders his son, his hand held threateningly in the air.

In the accompanying stunned silence, Dr Spicer jumps in with a query.

"How did you lose your eye, Mr Nathaniel?" she asks, obviously more interested in medical matters than introductions and small talk. "In some kind of a mining accident, I suppose?"

She has walked over to the counter and firmly placed a large, black, medical-looking bag on it, as if to assert herself.

"That's none of your business!" he roars. "A woman will be no doctor to *me*. And none of the folk of the town will come to see you either, I'll tell you that now. A woman doctor … it's unnatural!"

In the midst of the raised voices, I start to feel strange, still swaying from the journey, dizzy from bewilderment at the situation we have found ourselves in. I glance at Father, who gives me a nod, letting me know we shall be on our way just as soon as he can ask about the supplies we'll need.

"Yes, but you'll still have her board in your rooms at the back, as we agreed?" the mine manager asks the storekeeper.

"You expect me to stay *here*?" Dr Spicer bursts out.

"In what I suspect is a drinking den?"

I see her gaze at the long bench against the wall, at the barrel of liquor or beer that sits at the end of the counter.

"Ha! You will not be lodging here, madam, unless it's your wish to settle with four miners, myself and young Charlie."

"No, thank you. Isn't there a hotel or boarding house in town?" Dr Spicer turns and asks of the mine manager.

"The mining company have set up cabins for workers with families, as well as a dormitory building for the single men," Mr Eriksson replies with a frustrated flare of his nostrils. "There *is* nowhere else..."

"Except *your* home, Mr Eriksson," says the storekeeper, leaning his arms on the counter. "You surely have more than enough rooms in that fine house of yours."

"Now that's just not possible," says Mr Eriksson, waving his hand in a firm refusal. "Not with my wife ... the way she is. We can't have any disturbances."

"Oh, and what seems to be the problem with your wife?" asks Dr Spicer, her eyes like the persistent stare of a great horned owl behind her glasses.

Any answer given is lost to an awful sound – a sudden, muffled boom.

The deep, terrible rumble of it; I feel the very ground

ripple and move beneath my feet! And the shock of it seems to set off a sudden volley of coughing that consumes me, leaving barely room to draw breath.

The concerned face of Dr Spicer is the last thing I see before stars white as the snow outside whirl before my eyes – and all becomes dark.

CHAPTER 4

"O nam faicinn thu a' tighinn,
Ruithinn dhol nad chòdhail,
Ach mur tig thu 'n seo gam shireadh,
Ciamar thilleas dochas?

If I saw you coming,
I would run to meet you,
But if you don't come here to search for me,
How can hope return?"

When I open my eyes again, I am uncertain where I am, *or* why the words to "The Fairy Love Song" are ringing around in my head. I know only that something smells good.

For a moment, my heart surges, and think myself back in our fine stone cottage on Tornish. For Father is playing his tin whistle and a pot bubbles and hisses somewhere about the room.

"Ishbel? Effie?" I say, pushing myself up from some

kind of bed that I find myself resting on, a tangle of rough blankets covering me.

"Father, she's awake!" says Lachlan, staring at me, a halo of gold around his scruffy tufts of red hair.

The music of the whistle stills. And now Father rushes over, dropping to his knees on the floor beside me. "You are with us again at last, my Bridie?"

"What a fever you have had," Lachlan tells me excitedly. "You've been tossing and turning in a terrible, restless sleep for more than a *week*!"

"I-I remember a sound ... and the ground moved," I mutter.

"Oh, that was just an explosion!" says Lachlan, seeming so oddly light-hearted in his reply.

"An explosion?" I croak in my new-found, uncertain voice.

"It's all right; the miners set them off in the tunnels underground – to shake free rocks and find more seams of copper," my brother says matter-of-factly. "It happens every now and then. My friends say that you get used to it."

I blink at my brother, barely believing that could be possible.

"Now then, we made up a bed for you here, Bridie, so that we could easily watch over you," says Father, changing the subject as he gently lays a hand on my forehead. He smiles when he takes it away, clearly pleased with how he finds me.

"You're in the parlour, Bridie," says my brother, perhaps aware that I have no sense of where I am exactly. "And there are two small bedrooms through the back there, and the storefront is through *that* door. The privy is round the back, of course!"

"Slow down, Lachlan — your sister has only just opened her eyes," says Father, and I feel him take one of my hands and enclose it between his own work-roughened palms.

Still, I turn my head to the left to see one closed door, made of simple planks of wood, which must lead through to the storefront. I cannot focus my muddled mind on what the store might be exactly, but we seem to be in the living quarters behind it.

When I turn back to the kind and concerned faces of my brother and father, I notice behind them a window with a view of gently falling snowflakes, like a lace curtain that obscures any other view. Then there's a table and chairs, a stove, some shelves set with useful cooking things and some daintier things, and an embroidered picture pinned to the wall.

Lachlan notices where my gaze settles.

"Look — I put Mother's china dogs and good candlesticks and clock on the shelf there, along with Samuel's drawings. That one of you; you were at the top of the Glas Crags. Do you remember the Glas

Crags? The rocky hill on Tornish? Do you?"

Lachlan's words; they run as if they were in a race. I focus my eyes on the framed picture my chattering brother points at – and there I am, sitting on a large stone, long, black hair flying free in the wind, my gaze off to the west. Glas Crags, Tornish, Samuel – snatches of these names *almost* make sense, but I still don't know quite where I am and what is what.

"*Ist*, now, Lachlan," says Father, using the Gaelic word to try to quieten my excitable brother. "Let Bridie be."

"But so much has happened!" Lachlan continues like a puppy fussing over a fresh bone. "We were very worried for you because Dr Spicer said you had bronchitis, as well as the fever. But she has made you better, with poultices for your chest."

I look down below the neck of my nightdress and see there is some padded cloth wrapped around me, and a mix of strong smells that I cannot quite place.

"And Easter brought you chicken broth every day, and Father and I fed you a little on a spoon at a time, though you did not properly wake. It helped make you well again, didn't it? Do you want some more now? I can get some for you!"

"Lachlan…" Father says with a gentle warning in his voice as he helps me sit up on the makeshift bed.

"Oh, and it barely stops snowing here in Hawk's

Point." Lachlan chatters on regardless. "But I have got to know some of the children at the miners' camp... I have made friends with two German girls, Henni and Matilde. And I have a job, cleaning at the canteen and running errands for the workers."

"That's when he hasn't been here, helping look after you, Bridie," Father tells me. "He really has been a good lad and a good brother to you."

"Yes! I've been here when Father's been out talking to Mr Eriksson – he's to carry on the building work Mr Gillespie had started around the town. So we will be quite rich, even with the amount Mr Nathaniel charges at his store! And then, of course, there's the money Dr Spicer is paying us for rent..."

"Don't you listen to him, Bridie! We will have a good income but we won't be rich," says Father with a smile in his voice.

But I hardly hear what he says as my mind rattles with yet *more* names I've just heard: Mr Gillespie, Mr Eriksson, Mr Nathaniel, Dr Spicer... Who *are* all these people?

"Never mind money. How are you feeling, *m' eudail*?" Father asks me, tilting his head as he studies me, love and concern in his brown-eyed gaze.

But my mind is in the grip of a whirlwind, struggling to still and steady the ever-shifting names and faces coming into sharp focus and fluttering away again like gulls rising off the sea…

"I cannot be lying about here." I suddenly sit bolt upright and try to throw off the blankets. "There must be so much to do!"

"Quiet, now," Father says soothingly, gently pushing me back down on to the bed. "It'll be a while till you feel yourself, till you're strong again."

"But I am *always* strong!" I insist, trying to push myself straighter still, as a muddle of memories thrust and shove their way forward. "Did I not always beat Will when we raced to the top of the Glas Crags? And … and was I not strong when the new Laird was going to set the law on you and we had to flee from Tornish? And I was certainly strong the time I hid Lachlan from the police in Glasgow the day that…"

Father is still holding my arms but his expression is most peculiar. He appears embarrassed. His eyes seem set on something to the side of me.

"Bridie," Lachlan starts up again, as a woman's frowning face moves into view. "Do you remember Dr Spicer? She is lodging with us till Father can build her dispensary."

I freeze as I recognise the earnest, bespectacled woman from the steamship. Of course … I *do* remember her, and a store we were in and some angry men jabbering about her.

"Your daughter is clearly still a little confused because

of her fever," says Dr Spicer, seeming not to suspect that I was actually speaking the truth just now. "I'll go and make up a fresh poultice."

"And perhaps some coffee would be good," Father says quickly, rushing away before the doctor can see his flushed face. "I'll fetch fresh water from the barrel outside."

Dr Spicer hurries into one of the back rooms, shutting the door behind her, while Father opens a side door I have not noticed behind me, closing it to keep out the frost-edged air that tries to bluster its way in. And now left alone, my brother and I stare at each other.

"Bridie! You nearly told!" Lachlan hisses.

"Shh… I know!" I say back.

There is a Gaelic saying – *"Cha sgeul-rùin e 's fios aig triùir air"* – that means "It's not a secret if three people know it". But Father, Lachlan and I have managed very well these past two years to keep those darker secret things to ourselves, so I feel terrible for starting to say them out loud.

And yet … before I know it, my brother and I begin snickering, covering our mouths to stifle the noise. The effort of shushing the hiccupping, helpless laughter hurts my chest, but it is still wonderful to be silly when all has been so serious lately.

When our silliness ebbs away, I am a little steadier, a little more like my old self. And my old self knows that while I can take a moment to look fondly over my shoulder to the past, I must take a longer, steadier look to the future.

"So, what do you make of Hawk's Point, Lachlan?" I ask my brother, as I rest back against my pillows.

"I like it well enough. I'm earning money so that, when I am older and the war is over, I can go back to New York and work in a grand hotel."

A smile stays on my face, but a stab of sadness twinges in my chest as I think of our shrunken family shrinking any further.

"But you know people aren't happy here in town," he carries on. "Everyone is worried that the mine will fail before it has started. Easter says that the mine manager and Mr Nathaniel from the general store are always griping together about the lack of copper being dug out."

Easter – that name again. I'm about to ask who this Easter is when Lachlan leans forward with a grin and says the most peculiar thing.

"And everyone supposes there's a *curse* on the mine. What do you think to that, Bridie?"

"A curse?" I say, pushing myself up a little on the bed and grinning back at my brother. "I think it sounds like nonsense, but please tell me more – it sounds most entertaining."

"Well, folk think the ghost of a Chippewa maiden

haunts Hawk's Point," Lachlan says, his eyes wide at the telling of this tall tale. "They say she walks through the town at night in a great long, hooded cape made of black feathers!"

With that, my brother grabs my shawl from the end of the bed, puts it over his head and strides around the small parlour in a solemn fashion, failing miserably to mimic some scary spirit.

"What?" I laugh, making my chest burn a little with pain again. "Why would some poor, departed Indian woman waste her time wandering about in this little town?"

"They say that she has placed the curse on Hawk's Point because the mining company dares to dig up her ancestral lands," says Lachlan in a most theatrical tone. "They say the Chippewa Curse is the reason they can only find poor, thin seams of copper to mine."

I break into a smile, remembering some of the superstitions many Highlanders believed – our sister Effie included. Witches that would steal milk from the cows, elf-bolts that would be shot at cattle to make them skittish, water bulls that live in lochs and shape-shifting, mischievous kelpies...

"You know my friend Henni?" Lachlan continues, flopping down beside me again, the shawl still gripped tight under his chin.

I nod in reply to his question, though I only heard

the girl's name a few minutes ago.

"Well, her brother Oskar says *he's* seen the spirit. He came across her one night up near the mine head. He's a grown lad of sixteen, but ever since, he won't go out after dark!"

"And the people here choose to believe him?" I ask in surprise.

"Oh, he's not the only one. There's quite a few folk that claim to have seen her, floating around near the mine head, disappearing and reappearing in amongst the trees…"

As a small child, I might have been deliciously chilled at the description of the eerie Indian spirit. But now the idea of a ghostly figure sounds like pure fancy that I simply can't—

"Oh!" I murmur in surprise, suddenly catching sight of my own reflection in the little mirror on the shelf by the china dogs.

Lachlan mistakes what has caught my eye. He hurries over to the shelf and picks up a small pot that holds several glossy black feathers, like a miniature bunch of dark blooms.

"These are *not* from the spirit's cloak, Bridie," he assures me. "They're only crow feathers I've been collecting. Aren't they beautiful?"

"Yes," I agree, as my brother swivels the pot in his fingers and the black of the feathers reveals shifting sheens of emerald green and deep sapphire blue. "But I was actually looking at the mirror…"

"Ha!" Lachlan chuckles, putting the pot down and grabbing the mirror instead. He brings it over to me, holding it up to my face.

"Well," I say, turning my head this way and that, the better to see the tangles of long, black hair that hang either side of my face and the dark hollows in my cheeks and below my eyes. "Looking the way I do, I think that if I wandered the town here after dark tonight, I could *quite* easily be mistaken for the ghost of the Indian maiden, don't you?"

Father and Dr Spicer both return from their separate errands and must wonder if they are in the right room. Because a few minutes ago they left a frail invalid and her worried brother, and now they have come back to two fools – one with a shawl over his head – laughing till the rafters shake…

CHAPTER 5

"HELLOOO!" shouts Lachlan.

"HELLOOO … hellooo … *hellooooo*!" comes the booming echo from the great, yawning hole in the side of the tree-covered hill, its sides and roof held up with walls of roughly planed timber.

"Oi! Get away from there, boy!" shouts one of the men working near the muddy, slushy mouth of the mine. His voice has a cheery, Irish lilt to it. "You're bothering the men at work below. They'll be wondering what all the shouting's about!"

"Sorry, Seamus," Lachlan says with a grin. "I was just showing my sister the pit."

"Fancy a job as a miner, do you, my dear?" The man winks at me as he sets off pushing a wheeled cart along a track towards some outbuildings.

Smiling, I shake my head in reply. I have been in the dark pit of illness recently, and it has taken me some time to clamber out of it, so I can think of nothing more awful than scrambling down endless ladders into candle-lit tunnels, only to spend the day hammering at rocks or setting those ground-rumbling explosions in the hope of finding pockets of precious copper.

"*Guten tag*, Lachlan!" an older boy's voice calls out, and I see a lanky lad in a cap hurry by us, ruffling my brother's hair as he goes.

"*Guten tag*, Oskar!" Lachlan replies cheerily, repeating the German word for hello.

"He said your name very well," I comment.

Since we came to America, my brother has found it funny *and* frustrating that folk can't make the rolling, back-of-the-throat, Scottish "ch" sound and mostly call him "Lacklan". But of course German folk use the "ch" sound in their own language.

"That's Oskar, my friend Henni's brother. He's just started to work in the mine alongside his father, though he wishes to enlist as a soldier in the Union Army in the spring when he can leave here," Lachlan chatters as the older lad walks away. "*And* he's taught me some card games."

"Not for money, I hope!" I say quickly, thinking of the bad lot he found for friends back in Glasgow. "You're not gambling, are you?"

"No! We only play for matchsticks or pebbles," he assures me, a little offended I think. "Oskar has no money – he gives whatever he earns to his mother. But anyway, come on – I'll take you to see the stables and then the mine canteen next."

My eleven-year-old brother has become quite at home here the last few weeks, while I've been convalescing in the living quarters at the back of the Gillespie carpentry store, watched over by Dr Spicer when she isn't poring over her piles of medical books behind the hung sheet that splits the small, back bedroom she and I share.

This morning – the first in a while with no blinding blizzard – Lachlan has shown me that there is not much to Hawk's Point at all. To walk from the harbour, along the main street, past the miners' lodging house and cabins, to the wooden buildings of the mine and the shaft itself ... it must take little more than a few minutes or so. And, more's the pity, there are no twinkling pebbles of pure copper to be seen in the snow-free pockets of frost-hardened earth we have come across... With nothing better to do, I go to follow my brother when I hear someone else call out to him.

"*Grüß dich*, Lachlan!"

I turn and there are two giggling young girls, wrapped tight in their shawls.

"Hello to you too," my brother calls back, pink creeping across his cheeks.

"So these are your new friends?" I say with a smile, watching my brother blush.

"Yes! The one with the darker hair is Henni; the other is Matilde."

"They look like nice girls," I tell him.

"They are! They're both teaching me German and I'm helping them with their English," Lachlan replies. "I'm teaching them some Gaelic too!"

It is quite obvious that my brother would like to give up being my guide and be with his friends right now. And truth be told, I would quite like to feel as if I am not an invalid any more.

"Stay awhile, Lachlan. I am happy to go back home now…"

I would also like to be away from the awful stamp mill. If the endless clanging of it drove me mad in my sickbed, it is a *hundred* times worse this close up.

"Are you sure, Bridie?" Lachlan asks me hopefully.

"I'm sure," I say and take my leave of him, heading along the rubbled road that leads back up through the cabins where the men with families live.

A little way behind the jumbled cabin roofs, the forest begins, clawing its way up the snowy banks at the bottom of the cliffs. No children play there; Father says the snow is so deep it would quickly engulf those that do not know their way into its puffy, suffocating bosom. The only creatures confident enough to prowl there are the wolves we hear howling at night, the prey they stalk, and the hunters who try and catch both wolves and prey with guns or metal-fanged traps.

There are smaller woods on the other side of the

road. Beyond them is the shore where, at this time of year, I have heard that careless children try stepping out on the ice of the great lake, till older, wiser folk urge them to return to welcoming arms and slaps for their recklessness.

But in amongst the trees here, I notice a larger wooden building standing in a clearing. It *has* to be the mine manager's house; it is better built than the plain and rough stores and cabins, or the long lodging house for the single men. For a start, it has two floors and a porch, not to mention fine-looking curtains at all the windows, when every other building in this town seems to have no cloth at its windows at all, including ours. It's not fancy by any means – nothing like the huge and ornate stone and brick-built houses in New York or Glasgow, or Mrs Lennox's grand villa where my sister Effie is a maid. (Or at least she *was*, last I knew.)

But this place must be, what, large enough for a decent parlour and kitchen? Two bedrooms upstairs, perhaps?

"It's Mr and Mrs Eriksson's place."

I jump a little, as if I've been caught spying.

"You look well, Miss Bridie," says the girl, who I recognise from that first day at the general store. The girl whose wrist was grabbed by the shopkeeper. The girl who brought chicken soup for me when I was in my fevered sleep.

"Please just call me Bridie," I say. "And yes, I am feeling well, thank you. And you are Easter, I think?"

Easter's eyes seem quite fixed on mine, as if she is trying to peer inside and read my mind, perhaps to see if I truly am better or not.

"It's my first time outside," I tell her. "I have just been to look at the mine."

"And I have just been to Nat's Store," says Easter, holding up her heavy wicker basket as proof.

"My, what a pleasure *that* must have been."

The mocking words are out of my mouth before I think better of it, but they are met with a broad smile, dimples appearing in Easter's dark, round cheeks. I expect Easter is not at *all* fond of the storekeeper. And she is not alone; Lachlan says he is despised by every one of the miners and their families. Yet come Saturday night, the menfolk of Hawk's Point somehow manage to swallow their dislike for the man and hand him their wages in exchange for beer or whiskey, perching on the bench inside his store or on the stoop outside to drink it. We easily hear the carousing, arguing and fighting, since the general store is directly across the main street from our building.

"Pity there's not a church built here yet," adds Easter, with a knowing lift of one eyebrow. "Mr Nathaniel could sure do with repenting his sins, I reckon."

We *both* smile broadly now, till a shy silence

trickles upon us.

"I should probably thank your ... I mean, Mr and Mrs Eriksson, for sending the chicken soup," I say, for *something* to say.

"Oh, they ... they don't really know," says Easter with a shake of her head. "Mrs Eriksson is an invalid; she leaves all the running of the house to me. And as for Mr Eriksson..."

"He is a busy man, I suppose?"

As I talk, I think to myself that Easter doesn't look old enough to be in charge of a whole house. She must only be a little younger than me, I suppose. I glance back at the house and wonder where she rests her head at night. Smart as it is, there's not space for a separate servant's room. I dare say Easter has a foldaway cot bed tucked in a nook in the kitchen.

"Yes, he's a busy man," Easter says, nodding thoughtfully. "*So* busy he often prefers to pass the time of day with Mr Nathaniel, instead of being at the mine or at his desk. And *so* busy he has not remembered my name since he employed me in Chicago six months ago. He still calls me Hester!"

I cannot help laughing at a supposedly *clever* man's stupidity. Easter laughs too, till she seems to remember herself, glancing down towards the house in the trees.

"I'd better go," she says.

"Your mistress, she is strict?" I ask her.

"No – well, she *tried* to be at the beginning, but not any more. We rub along well enough," Easter says with an easy shrug. "Anyway, she'll be asleep for hours yet. It's just that *Mr* Eriksson might come along this way and *he* won't like to see me idling."

I give Easter a nod as she takes her leave of me and set off too, towards the main street. All the while, curiosity is flitting around in my mind, making me feel more alert than I have in weeks.

What illness might Mrs Eriksson have that makes her a housebound invalid? As for Easter; I have heard of Chicago – it's a good way south of here, south of the Great Lakes in fact. Is all her family still there? There are times when I feel sad at how small *my* family has become. Yet how must Easter bear it, being, what, thirteen or fourteen, here in the Upper Peninsula of Michigan, so far from anywhere with no kin at all? I cannot imagine how it must feel to be so alone.

"Ah, just the girl!"

I turn at the sound of Father's voice and see him standing at the skeleton of a building, which is to be a school from the spring, when a teacher should arrive on the first ship of the year. Father wields a saw in one hand as he continues the carpentry work that Iain Gillespie started. From our evening talks in the warmth of the parlour, I know that Father has postponed the work on the dispensary for Dr Spicer, as there is no place in town to buy a stove for it. So Dr Spicer is to set to stay with us till spring, even though a lone woman living under Father's roof has caused some raising of eyebrows from those who think it slightly scandalous.

"So, what do you make of Hawk's Point, then, Bridie?" Father asks with a smile. "It quite rivals New York in its splendour, does it not?"

"Indeed, Father!" I reply to his merrymaking. "Once the miners hit a great seam of copper, the town will become *very* wealthy and fashionable, I'm sure. Perhaps Mr Barnum will seek to open another of his museums here!"

"Now wouldn't that be something," Father says jovially, though there is a flicker of a frown at the mention of that place and the memory of the event that happened there. "But until the town has museums and promenades and all manner of entertainments, there *is* a way *you* can help pass the time for some of the townsfolk, Bridie."

"Me?" I say with a frown of my own.

"Dr Spicer has had an idea… She's back at the store – go see her. She'll explain everything."

I must look confused, or wary – or a mixture of both. Father shoots me a questioning look.

"It's just that … well, I am a little unsure of Dr Spicer," I tell him, feeling foolish as soon as the words leave my mouth. But it's true; during this time of my recovery I have barely had a conversation with her, beyond basic pleasantries and questions and instructions to do with my health. I'm certainly awkward when she bandages the nightly warmed poultice of mustard and potassium nitrate around my bare chest...

A shadow passes over Father's face.

"Dr Spicer has devoted herself to her studies the last few years," he says. "She may not indulge in idle chit-chat like many others, but she cares deeply about science and medicine, and the difference it can make to people's lives..."

It may be that she has, but so far, Dr Spicer has had not *one* patient seek her out. Not because folk are remarkably healthy in Hawk's Point, but because – as Mr Nathaniel said that first day – none of them will trust a woman to do a man's job. Even Mr Eriksson has rebuffed her enquiries about the well-being of his never-seen wife.

"And Dr Spicer is brave, learning a profession people think not suitable for her sex," Father continues, as if he has read my thoughts. "She is brave too because she is recently widowed and has decided to come to a place like this, on her own. She is brave because she doesn't care what people think is possible or right for a woman to do. She just does it."

Now I feel thoughtless as well as foolish.

"Sorry, Father," I tell him. "I'll go to her straightaway."

"Good lass," Father replies, with warmth returning to his face.

Lifting my skirts from the mire of the slush and dampened earth, I hurry back to Gillespie's store, wondering what Dr Spicer has in mind for me – and readying myself to be polite and enthusiastic whatever she bids me do, for Father's sake.

As I approach the building, I notice that the front door of the place is wedged open. Earlier, Lachlan and I left by the side door, as that leads straight to the back half of the building where our living quarters are. This larger space, the shop-front of the building, is full of the tools and planed timber and suchlike that Mr Gillespie will sell here when he returns in the spring.

"Hello!" I say shyly, knocking at the open door.

"Bridie! How has your first outing been?" asks Dr Spicer. She has the sleeves of her shirt rolled up. The waistcoat she wears, like her coat, is mannish, but it looks loose and comfortable, unlike the nipped-in, tight clothing most well-to-do women wear. For the first time, I try to guess what her age might be. About thirty years, perhaps?

"Fine, thank you," I answer her, nodding and gazing around the large square room. It seems bigger. The wood and tools Mr Gillespie stored here are being shifted to one side, it seems. But to what purpose?

"Good, good," Dr Spicer says briskly, blowing a

strand of loosened, dark brown hair away from her face. "Now, Bridie, I've heard that you taught basic letters and numbers to a small child back in New York. Is that correct?"

My polite smile fades as I think sorrowfully of my little companion, Marthy-Jane. "Yes, I did."

"So we will set up a schoolroom here," says Dr Spicer, "until such time as the schoolhouse is built and a teacher appointed."

"I-I see," I stammer, though I am not entirely sure I *do* see.

"School will run in the morning, leaving afternoons free for me to see patients – when they choose to come. *I* will teach the older children and *you* will teach the young ones," says Dr Spicer, all of a sudden making her meaning *more* than plain to me. "What do you say?"

I can say nothing; I am struck dumb. At fifteen – and after everything my family have been through – I do not feel much like a child any more. But I am hardly a grown woman ready to take on such a role! And when did a lowly crofter's daughter ever become a teacher?

"Excuse me," a voice interrupts from behind, and I stand aside as Jean walks in bearing a bench made from a plank. "This all right, Miss?"

His dog stops at the door and turns its thickly furred body in a circle before settling on the wooden floorboards. Odayan looks comfortable but keeps a keen eye on his master.

"Perfect. Thank you, Jean. Can you make me two, no, three more of those, please? And some basic long tables too? Just when you have time between your other jobs."

With the business of the school furniture settled, Dr Spicer turns her attention back to me.

"Naturally, we can teach more than just reading and writing and arithmetic, Bridie," she says, as she grabs hold of a long, wrapped roll of roofing tar paper and begins to drag it across the room. I grab the other end of the heavy roll, beating Jean to it. "There's science and medicine, of course. And as for politics, well, we can talk about our wonderful President Lincoln and discuss the Civil War, and the injustice of the slavery system in the south. In fact, *you* could tell the pupils about the terrorist attack in New York, Bridie! And we could ask the children to recount why their own families came to America – whether it was due to poverty or religious persecution or war in their homeland – that would be a good introduction to geography, wouldn't it?"

I cannot keep up with Dr Spicer. She may not be one for common small talk, but when it comes to bookishness and learning, her mind seems to sprint, fuelled by science, while mine lags behind, filled as it has been by laundry work and chicken feed the last two years.

"And it doesn't have to be just the children talking about where their families originally hail from," Dr Spicer continues. "The mine manager and his wife are from Sweden... Perhaps I can persuade him to join us too!"

"The *wife* is not Swedish," Jean interrupts. "I heard her speak when she arrived in the summer. I think she is from England."

Dr Spicer blinks, taking in this new information about the mine manager's wife. "You have met her? What is she like? Was she poorly when she arrived?"

"I only saw her a time or two," Jean replies with another of his shrugs. "Seemed pretty young. Looked skinny and pale."

I think I am as intrigued by this solitary, sick person as Dr Spicer clearly is. Dr Spicer's interest might be that of a doctor thinking of someone's physical health, but I simply find it sad to think of anyone being locked away indoors and lonely...

"Anyway, Jean, we must of course have *you* talk to the pupils," Dr Spicer announces, changing the subject as the young man rearranges some gleaming new shovels and hoes to make space for the tar-paper roll. "You can tell us about the first people of this land — how does your tribe say it?"

"*All* tribes say it: *Anishinaabe*," says Jean, repeating the word I heard him use on the day we arrived.

LITTLE BIRD LANDS

"Yes, you can tell all the children about the *Anishinaabe* and your customs."

"I don't think there's many people in the town that would care to hear that," says Jean darkly.

Dr Spicer takes the weight of the tar-paper roll from me and props it up against the wall. "The American Declaration of Independence clearly states that all men are born equal, Jean. Now some of the older residents of Hawk's Point might struggle to remember that sometimes, but let's at least try and make sure the *children* understand that fully, shall we?"

Jean does not seem convinced, but at least gives Dr Spicer a nod and a shrug.

And now she's addressing me again.

"Bridie, I've heard that the mining company delivered a parcel of slates and pencils to Mr Nathaniel's store back in the summer, in readiness for the school being built. Can you fetch them sometime? I think we should aim to start in a week or two. Perhaps after Christmas. A new term for the new year!"

At last, I find my voice.

"I-I am not sure I can..." I stumble.

"I'm sorry?" says Dr Spicer, her stare intense behind the wire-rim circles of her spectacles.

"What I mean is, I don't think I can teach all those children," I tell her. "I don't know enough to do it."

"Don't be silly, Bridie," Dr Spicer says matter-of-factly, brooking no refusal. "You've been to school yourself. You seem intelligent and sensible and will be more than capable of following my lead. So what on earth can stop you doing whatever you set your mind to?"

I am confounded by Dr Spicer's bossy tone at first. But as soon as I see past that and make sense of what she has said, I feel a bloom grow in my chest, in my heart; a bloom that tingles in my veins and explodes in my head.

Her words, they sound like freedom. And there *was* a time I dreamt of freedom, back on the island, back on Tornish. I'd lie on the moss at the top of the Glas Crags, staring up at the sea eagles soaring in the cloud-stacked sky above, wondering what it might be like to be a girl who could *go* where she wanted and *be* whatever she pleased. But that carefree thought has lain buried inside me for the longest time now.

Till now.

Perhaps I am no longer lucky enough to have my mother, my sisters, the friendship of Will. But I am lucky enough to have myself and that is sufficient. I am Bridie MacKerrie, and nothing can stop me doing whatever I set my mind to.

Nothing.

LITTLE BIRD LANDS

I rush over to a plainly surprised Dr Stephanie Spicer, because right at this minute, hugging her is what I have set my mind to...

CHAPTER 6

I waken to a soft, bright quietness outside and a warm tinkle of voices and breakfast things within.

The hay-filled mattress rustles softly as I toss aside my blankets, clamber out of bed and pitter-patter on cold tiptoes to the window. And wonderfully, there has been a pause to the endless snow; the piercing blue skies and butter-yellow sunlight – so dearly missed in the daily, swirling blanket of white – are like a gift for the eyes. And another gift is the silence … for this morning the stamp mill is thankfully stilled. Not because it is Sunday and a day of rest, but because it is Christmas. A day when the miners' wives might make a bit of a better meal for their families than the usual carefully rationed salted bacon, stew and skillet-fried biscuits.

I hurry out of my thick nightdress and into my warm layers of skirt, flannel petticoat, shirt, knitted jumper, stockings and shawl. But before I leave the bedroom, I pause by the hanging sheet that separates my half of the room from Dr Spicer's. My half has the window and door, and hers ... well, I don't know what it looks like. I've been curious, of course, but always too polite – or too scared – to peek. But this morning, the doctor is clearly not there; I have heard the muffled sound of her voice through in the parlour. And the sheet, it does not fall straight today; it hangs a little to one side. Perhaps I might dare a swift glance...?

And so, breath held, I part the sheet a little further and stare into the private space behind it. The bed has been neatly made, as I would expect of Dr Spicer. A trunk and several bags are stacked at the end of it. Her dresses and skirts and coat are hung on roughly carved wooden pegs mounted on the wall. Above her bed there are two stout shelves, the upper laden with jars and thick glass demijohns with curious names written upon their labels: 'SALTS', 'CASTOR OIL', 'QUININE', 'CALOMEL', 'DOWNER'S STANDARD COUGH MEDICINE', 'MORPHINE', 'LINIMENT' and more.

On the lower shelf are many leather-bound books, a prettily shaped kerosene lamp, and something I have seen photographers on the streets of New York offer – a tintype photograph. I take a step closer and gaze at a gentleman's head and shoulders printed on to the thin metal plate, set inside a varnished wooden frame. The gentleman's oiled hair is combed close to his head, and he sports a bushy moustache and a serious but kindly expression. So this must be Dr Spicer's dear departed husband, I suppose?

A sudden ripple of laughter from the parlour makes me jump and remember my manners. I don't want to be caught and I don't want Dr Spicer to think ill of me... I have been enjoying our talks about what to teach once our make-do school opens. I am still in awe and a little shy of her however, and I have *certainly* not made a repeat of the hug I gave her not so long ago. The hug rather shocked us both, I think...

With a quick flick of the sheet "curtain" to neaten it, I turn, hasten through the door and see what is going on in the room beyond.

"Bridie! Look what we have made!" says Lachlan. He sits at the table with silver scissors in one hand and a piece of old newspaper in the other. But he is pointing towards Dr Spicer, who is fixing a length of twine, laden with lop-sided paper stars, to the wall by the window. The other walls are similarly ornamented.

"Lachlan was telling me that Christmas was not much celebrated back on your Scottish island," says Dr Spicer. "But in my hometown of Philadelphia, it has become quite the fashion to have decorations, as they do in Germany. In fact, the Germans also take trees into their homes and—"

In that instant the side door whacks wide open, battering against the wall. And there stands Father, grinning, one thickly gloved hand holding the trunk of a small fir tree across one shoulder, the other clutching an axe.

"I just met a couple of Irish fellows hunting for rabbits in the woods for their Christmas dinner. We got to talking and decided that while the weather's fine, we will have ourselves a gathering by the miners' cabins, with music and dancing!" he announces, thudding the tree up against the wall, and hurrying over to the shelf where his tin whistle lies. "So hurry – get your coats and warm things…"

For a heartbeat or two, the surprise announcement makes Lachlan, Dr Spicer and myself pause … then in another heartbeat or two we are rushing around in a frenzy of activity.

Though *I* will not be doing any dancing today, I think to myself just a short while later as I settle myself on a tree stump on the edge of the clearing by the miners' cabins. I will admit it to no one, but I don't quite trust my legs just yet; since my illness the muscles of my twisted foot in particular are weaker than I would wish. So while back at home on Tornish I would dance as long and as hard as anyone else at gatherings in the island's townships, this morning I am content to watch as the men, women and children of Hawk's Point whoop and whirl, whether they are Cornish or Scottish, German or Irish or Yankee, whether they are familiar with the tunes or not.

It takes a minute or two to realise there is someone

by my side. It is the tongue-lolling panting of his companion that gives Jean away.

"Your father plays well," he says, giving a simple flick of the hand that has Odayan obediently lying flat down on the hard, snow-packed ground.

As he crouches down beside me, I notice that Jean's heavy, worn black coat hangs open and I catch a glimpse of the colourful beadwork of his belt once again. I would *so* like to learn how to make something that beautiful. How pleasant it would be to pass the dull, winter evenings here making such a thing instead of darning socks and stockings!

"Yes," I agree to Jean's compliment to Father's whistle skills. "But you should hear him play the bagpipes."

I wonder who has Father's set now? We had to flee Tornish with so little that he gifted his precious pipes to one or other of our neighbours.

"Bagpipes?" says Jean, turning to me with a quizzical look on his face.

I struggle to think how I might explain the *pìob mhòr*... Do I tell him the bare facts of it, that it is a bag made of the hide of an animal, wooden blow-sticks and windpipes attached to it? Or do I let him know the Great Highland Bagpipe is beloved and much revered back home, with such a powerful, haunting sound to it that can make your heart soar to a stirring march played upon it, or just as easily bring you to tears with a sorrowful lament? In this moment I can say neither, for a clear memory is come to me, of the time my friend Will fell backwards on to his brother George's set of pipes, and the escaping wind sounded near enough like the tortured groans of a dying beast. I cannot tell you how long Will and I helplessly laughed for…

"It is an instrument of my homeland," I say simply instead, trying to stop a smile in case Jean thinks I am laughing at him.

Luckily, his own gaze is on the Irish lads and their handheld *bodhrán* drums. "We use drums and singing for our dances," he says.

At the mention of his people, I take the opportunity to ask Jean something that confuses me.

"Why is it you have a French name, and not an Indian one?"

"There have been French–Canadian traders and trappers and missionaries in this land for many, many years, since before my grandfather's own grandfather's time," he answers. "Some married *Anishinaabe* women. Some French names took hold."

"So the French that first went to Canada, they travelled south here long before any of the rest of us travelled across the sea to America?" I ask.

Jean nods. "Yes, but there were not so many of them. Now there are many, *many* more of you. White people are coming like a sea; like waves and waves that never stop…"

I feel sick, suddenly realising that myself, Father and Lachlan are part of that unstoppable wave.

"I'm … I'm so sorry that your people are being made to share your land," I tell him, my words sincere though they might sound shy and awkward.

"There is no *sharing*, miss," Jean says sharply. "There is just taking."

I halt for a moment, then try to explain how it has been for folk from the Highlands and Islands for the past century.

"Jean, I *do* understand about land being taken," I say. "Where I'm from in Scotland, hundreds of thousands of poor families have been cleared off their farms, left homeless and desperate by landlords who care not how they survive. It goes on still – it is why we come to countries such as this to start new lives…"

"Yes, but then for *your* people to have new lives, is it fair that *my* people lose our old lives?" Jean counters, sounding weary and not angry, though he has every right to be.

"But I thought tribes were given money by the government to move to reservations?" I say.

"Money that is often never paid," says Jean. "Moved to land that is often so poor it is impossible to farm or hunt on…"

Despite the joyful jigs and reels going on only a few

feet away, my heart suddenly aches. For all of us who have left dire situations in our homelands for a better life, it means someone *else's* life must become much worse. I find myself ashamed that I've not properly understood this till now.

"What are they dancing for?" Jean suddenly asks me, perhaps sensing my discomfort and so, very kindly, not letting me suffer it.

"To celebrate Christmas Day," I tell him, gulping down my difficult thoughts. "Do you know of that?"

"Uh-huh," Jean mutters, his eyes on the crowd, a glint of curiosity in his eyes. "In the town down the coast I have heard people sing together for Christmas. Their songs sounded serious and sad. I have never seen white people dance like this, like they are full of joy."

Full of joy, and a fair few of them full of ale very soon. On the far side of the crowd I have already caught sight of Mr Eriksson, as stern-faced as usual, feeling duty-bound to take part in his workforce's celebration. He must have organised the ale to be brought down from the general store – Henni's lanky brother Oskar is rolling a rattling barrel down the road, followed by Mr Nathaniel himself – but his gesture obviously brings Mr Eriksson no pleasure.

I've seen Easter too, a large shawl wrapped tight around her as she walks amongst the watching, foot-tapping audience, offering biscuits from a large plate.

"My father says that the music will also give some cheer to everyone in town," I carry on, feeling the weight of Odayan's hairy head rest on my booted feet. "It'll take them away from the gloom of this hard winter, he says, and their worries about the mine being jinxed."

"Jinxed?" Jean checks my meaning again.

"Having bad luck wished upon it," I try to explain. "The mine is not producing enough copper, and the folk here think it is cursed."

"The mine is *not* cursed," Jean mutters. "And maybe they're mining in the wrong places..."

"What do you mean?" I look up at him and ask.

"People mined here in ancient times. You can still see traces of the places they dug for copper. Large hollows in the forest floor show the places of their mine heads, if you know where to look."

"And do you?" I ask.

"Maybe, maybe not," he says with another of his shrugs. "But I'm not here to help the white men. I'm here to work hard and make money for my family."

"And what of the curse folk chatter about?" I ask, bending over without thinking to ruffle the ears of Odayan, the way I would our old pup Patch. "The Indian maiden with her cape of black feathers that some have seen by the mine...?"

Jean notices the dog's obvious pleasure, its head

tilting back towards my hand, its steely grey eyes softly closing. Its trust in me appears to settle something; Jean must surely trust me too, for in the next moment, he tells me a startling truth.

"That fool Nat – I was in his store one morning last summer. He was shaken up. Said he'd seen a dark shadow hovering up by the mine the night before, same as many others had. He must have been drunk on his own ale. He asked me if it could be an Indian spirit."

"And you told him it was?" I ask.

"No. I just did *this*," says Jean, giving one of his usual shrugs. "It was up to *him* to think about my meaning."

"And he must have decided yes?" I suggest.

"Huh." Jean gives a little laugh. "And then he told others, and the story took hold, growing and growing!"

I break into a grin. Mr Nathaniel has let himself be tricked, like a boy duped in a schoolyard game of whispers, without Jean saying a single word...

"Excuse me, Bridie?" I suddenly hear a voice call out urgently to me.

Easter is hurrying towards us, Lachlan's friends Henni and Matilde by her side.

"These girls say your brother is gone to cause trouble at my master's house," Easter announces.

"Lachlan?" I say disbelievingly.

"Charlie said we must all go with him," Henni babbles fast, "to look in the window of the manager's house for the mistress, while no one else was home."

"We would not go, but he takes hold of Lachlan like *this*," Matilde joins in, demonstrating on her friend, grabbing at her sleeve. "He says to Lachlan it is a dare. That he is a *coward* not to go."

"Yes, so Lachlan, he goes with him!" Henni adds.

My blood begins to boil, thinking of Charlie's teasing, of how very stupid my brother is to rise to it.

"I don't care for Mr Nathaniel's son, but I reckon your brother is a good enough boy. So I thought I'd come to *you* and not Mr Eriksson," says Easter.

Handing her plate of biscuits to the younger girls to distribute, Easter turns to leave, clearly expecting me to follow.

"Thank you," I say, disturbing Odayan as I get up and hurry after her.

The folk that are dancing and watching are having too good a time of it to take any notice of the two of us darting off among the jumble of cabins – our worn boots slithering and skittering across the lumpen, iced-up road – before hurrying down the way through the trees to the Eriksson's place.

"Can you see them?" I ask Easter.

"No," she says, looking from the front of the large wooden house to the clusters of tall pines standing guard on either side of it.

"What can they be thinking?" I say in despair.

LITTLE BIRD LANDS

"I don't suppose they are thinking very hard at all," says Easter, her deep dark eyes fixed more on *me* than seeking out the lads. "They are just come to gawp at the mad woman they suppose her to be."

"And she is not? Mad, I mean?" I can't help but ask, as we get closer.

"No. She suffers from melancholy, and her head pains her greatly – the noise of the stamp mill causes it," Easter explains. "She takes a draught to help her sleep through the day, till the clatter stops as evening sets in."

Melancholy... I have heard of that. It is a wretched sadness of the soul, I think. I'd feel sorry for anyone suffering from it, even if they *are* a well-off young woman sitting at her ease in a fine house.

"I hear your mistress is from England," I say, as a suggestion comes to me. "Maybe I could call on her sometime, since I'm from Scotland, making us practically neighbours, back in Britain! Perhaps it would cheer her to talk of home?"

"Think she's too low and ashamed of her condition to have anyone visit her," says Easter. "As for Mr Eriksson – he's *definitely* ashamed of her. Can't see him ever allowing visitors."

I want to ask her more, but as we come to the side of the house I hear a hissed conversation coming from around the back of the building.

Naturally I ready myself to surprise and shoo away

the boys up to no good. But then Easter quickly holds tight to my arm and holds a finger to her lips. For it is *not* my brother and Charlie who I nearly pounced upon. The voices are deeper – and troubled.

"This is the *only* way. D'you hear me, Eriksson?" comes an unpleasant growl that is near all-American, but with a faint burr of Scots.

"I just don't know, Nathaniel…" we hear the mine manager reply in his more-halting Scandinavian accent. "It's too risky. Perhaps we should do nothing. Maybe I need to wait and consult with the mining company in the spring."

"You're saying you want to wait till the snows melts, to get a message down the coast to them?" I hear Mr Nathaniel ask sharply. "For gawd's sake, Eriksson, by that time it'll be too late! They'll take one look at how little copper's been mined here and shut the place down. *You'll* be ruined, *I'll* be ruined. And I'm too old and tired to start somewhere new."

"But the risk—"

"But there'll be no risk! I'll train the fella myself."

"Yes, but who do you have in mind?" Mr Eriksson asks, a nervous edge of uncertainty in his voice.

"Let *me* take care of that. I have my eye on someone…" Mr Nathaniel says darkly, sounding like a bear who's spied a salmon and is about to scoop it from the river. "And in the meantime, be a man for once –

just give me the money and I'll make it happen!"

There's a silence, and from the lack of argument it seems the storekeeper has bullied the mine manager into his way of thinking – whatever that is.

Then the silence is replaced by the stamp of feet and Easter and I glance at each other in dread and panic, knowing there's nowhere to run, nowhere to hide.

Any second now the two men will discover us, thinking we're deliberately listening in to their private conversations. And what that will mean for us, for Easter and her master in particular, I cannot say...

But the crunching footsteps begin to recede and we realise – with shoulder-sinking relief – that Mr Eriksson and Mr Nathaniel have left around the *other* side of the house.

"Come," whispers Easter, pulling me around to the rear of the building, so that we are quite hidden, should either of the men choose to turn and look back upon the place as they walk down the path to rejoin the celebrations.

"What was that about, do you think?" I whisper back, placing a hand on my chest to try and quiet my frantically beating heart.

"I don't know," says Easter, looking upon the two cigar butts carelessly tossed on the ground near the woodpile, and kicking snow over their burning embers.

And then a tiny movement catches in the corner of

my eye. A movement *inside* the house. I turn sharply to look through the nearby window and see into a large parlour, as wide as the whole building. The movement is the flicker of a fire in the grate, but the light of it shows the figure of a woman reclining on a sofa, draped in a floor-skimming, colourfully patterned silk robe. She faces the window to the front of the house, waving reed-thin arms in the air in time to the jigs that can be heard playing down by the cabins. From this angle, I can't quite make her out unless I move a little closer and squint so that—

"I think you should go," I hear Easter say sharply.

Immediately, I feel my cheeks flush red. Who knows where my brother and Charlie have gone; perhaps they saw the men and thought better of their foolish plan. But now *I* am the one who is guilty of shamefully spying on the poor lady inside!

"I'm sorry," I say, gathering up my skirts and hurrying away.

As I run, I realise I *had* hoped Easter and I might be friends. But it seems my curiosity just ruined the friendship before it even started...

CHAPTER 7

BOOM!

My heart is having quite the time of it.

Today is the first day I teach school. And mirroring the nerves I already feel, the ground now shudders beneath my feet as an underground blast from the mine loosens the rocks and their copper lode deep below.

But I give myself a shake and hold my chin up. The blasting is done; there'll not be another explosion for a few days now. As for teaching school, I can do this. Dr Spicer and Father have faith in me. I have faith in myself. And I have tied and pinned my hair up as neatly as I can, and wear my best skirt and jacket. Hopefully, this will make me appear more grown-up, someone children might listen to.

But it seems my hopes are to be dashed.

"Come away in," I say to the three latecomers lurking outside the door.

They stare at me, as if I have said something in a language they don't understand.

"You know, you are very *little* to be a teacher," Charlie Nathaniel challenges me as he hovers at the doorway of the store, showing off to the two lads by his side. It is clear from his swaggering manner that he enjoys the fact that he is a little taller than me...

"And *you*, Charlie," I say, as sternly as I can, "are a very big fellow to be so stupid as to leave the door wide open and let the heat slip out. Get inside, all of you, quickly."

To my surprise, Charlie and his friends do as they are told. And with the boys in and door slammed, we are all here. Most of the children already arrived are the youngest in the town, excited at the notion of having something different to do since every day in wintry Hawk's Point is the same, with the deafening heartbeat of the stamp mill ticking away the endless minutes and hours.

The younger children – who will be in *my* care – are seated at the long table placed closest to the heat of the stove in the corner. Of the older children to be taught by Dr Spicer, there is Lachlan, of course, as well as the two sweet German girls he *used* to call friends. Charlie's Christmas Day plan to spy on Mrs Eriksson never happened because at the last minute Charlie decided it was more fun to try to steal ale with his *other* friends – but the damage was done. Sensible Henni and Matilde have not yet forgiven my brother after he chose Charlie and a prank over them and good sense. Lachlan has taken that badly, but he was at least relieved that Henni's brother Oskar still takes time to ruffle his hair whenever he sees him.

I frown at Lachlan now, seeing him yawn rudely.

"Sorry!" he mouths at me. He has been up early, running morning errands for the miners before school. Even Mr Nathaniel had a task for my brother, giving him a package to take to Oskar and paying Lachlan with not a coin but with a piece of liquorice for his trouble. (I bet Charlie was too lazy to do it for his father – and not impressed with the payment of something he could help himself to anytime he wanted!)

Still, I smile a little as I see some new black crow feathers tucked in the top pocket of my brother's jacket; more for his strange collection kept in the pot on the shelf in our parlour! But then I am altogether distracted by some noisy clatter as Charlie and the two Irish lads settle themselves at another long table.

"Settle down!" says Dr Spicer, as she writes her pupils' names on a register.

The three boys quieten, but only because they have noticed Jean sitting on a stool in the corner where he oils some piece of leatherwork, Odayan lying at his feet. The dog feigns sleep I think – he sprawls at his ease, yet his pale eyes are surely open very slightly, his ears twitching, almost as if he is listening to the sudden rustle of whispering coming from Charlie and his cronies. I cannot think that they will be saying anything good or kind about his master. Yet they have no idea that Jean is an invited guest. He told Dr Spicer that he would like to observe what the children learn so that he might add to his own knowledge, and she was more than delighted to have him in the classroom.

"Welcome to school, everyone," says Dr Spicer, standing between the two groups of pupils and bidding me join her. "Before we begin our lessons, I thought we should be *properly* introduced to one another. So I'll start. My name is Dr Spicer, and I—"

"Please!" says Morwen, a little Cornish girl, raising her hand. "Do we call you 'doctor' or 'ma'am'?"

"You can call me ma'am, if you wish," Dr Spicer replies and seems about to continue when Charlie pipes up.

"If you're a *ma'am* and not a *miss*, it means you're married. So where's your husband?" he demands, looking around as if *Mr* Spicer might be hiding somewhere in the room.

"He died shortly before I came here to Michigan, as a result of a riding accident," Dr Spicer replies in her usual measured tone of voice, though I notice she seems to hold herself tighter and taller as the children gasp their surprise at how recent her husband's loss is.

It seems a kindness and a necessity to step in.

"Dr Spicer is from Philadelphia," I say brightly. "She trained at one of only two schools of medicine for women in the *whole* of America."

I expect the children to be suitably impressed. It seems they are not.

"Yes ... but you are not a *real* doctor, I think, ma'am?" says Matilde.

"I certainly am," says Dr Spicer, seeming to take no offence.

"You can't be, or you wouldn't be teaching school," Charlie butts in again.

"I have decided to teach school for a short time till a proper teacher is appointed."

"*And* because no one will come to you for doctoring, seeing as you're a *woman*," adds one of the older Irish lads.

"Well, that's just stupid!" Lachlan bursts in. "'Cause Dr Spicer helped my sister get well from bronchitis, didn't she?"

"Yeah, but she didn't fix her crooked hand or foot, or nothin'," Charlie whispers to his friends behind his hand, though it is not a whisper at all.

Heat rushes to my cheeks. I want to snap at Charlie for his ignorance!

"Charlie!" I hear Dr Spicer say, but before she can say more my *own* tongue runs away with me.

"There is nothing to fix when it comes to my hand

or foot," I announce, my blood practically at boiling point. "I was born this way, it causes me no discomfort and I manage very well, thank you."

"Well said, Miss MacKerrie," Dr Spicer adds. "Now, let's get on with—"

"If you *are* a doctor, ma'am, why don't you make Mrs Eriksson well?" Henni pipes up, innocently enough. "The lady is *so* poorly and does not ever leave her house."

In that moment, I feel my cheeks redden again at the memory of catching sight of Mrs Eriksson through her window.

"I would certainly do my best to help Mrs Eriksson if she came to me as a patient," I hear Dr Spicer reply diplomatically. "Anyway, let's—"

"My ma says she heard that the mine manager's wife can't walk or talk," another of the little children interrupts excitedly. Another chimes in and then the voices become a torrent, overlapping each other.

"She must have walked once. *My* ma remembers seeing her when they arrived last summer. Says she saw Mrs Eriksson sitting on her porch a time or two and then she disappeared."

"My pa heard she went quite mad and is strapped to her bed!"

"*My* pa said she saw the ghost of the Indian woman that put the curse on the mine, and *that's* what drove her mad with fear!"

I look to Jean and see he gazes down upon his work still – but I make out his eyebrow arch at the mention of the phantom we both know exists only in the townsfolk's fevered imaginations.

"Well, *my* pa thinks Mrs Eriksson's been murdered and buried in the garden!"

"Children … be quiet. BE QUIET!" Dr Spicer orders them, and stillness comes back to the room. Till Charlie calls out again.

"What's *she* doing here?" he asks, pointing to the front of the store and wrinkling his freckled nose in what looks awfully like disgust.

The door has been silently cracked open and Easter stands just a little way inside it, as if she is afraid she might not be permitted to enter.

"Hello there, Easter!" Dr Spicer says brightly. "Would you like to join us?"

Easter nods and slides her way in, closing the door soundlessly behind her.

I have not seen Easter since the day of the Christmas gathering. Constant snowstorms have played their mischievous games these last three weeks, confining everyone to home that did not have to work outside of it. I am a little shy to see her, considering last time we set eyes on each other I was hurrying away from the Eriksson's place, feeling foolish. But now she gives me the smallest of smiles and I wonder if I might consider myself forgiven?

"Lachlan, make room for Easter, please," Dr Spicer says to my brother. He dutifully moves up with a welcoming smile, letting Easter take her place beside him.

"But she can't be here!" Charlie blurts out. "She's a–a—"

"A girl who would like to learn? I think *that's* what you're trying to say, young man." Dr Spicer challenges him.

Charlie blushes. He wasn't going to say that at all. He was probably going to say a word that Dr Spicer did not care to hear.

"She's a servant," he grumbles instead, not wanting to be totally silenced in front of his snickering friends. "And *I'll* not be staying if the likes of *them* are here…"

With a sharp nod towards both Easter and Jean, Charlie swings his legs over the bench and takes his leave. Perhaps he hopes others will follow, but everyone – including the two Irish lads – keeps to their seat. The warmth and diversion of the makeshift school appears to hold their interest more than Mr Nathaniel's sulky son.

"Well, we've wasted quite enough time on nonsense," says Dr Spicer, walking over and closing the door behind the departing Charlie. "So let's dispense with the introductions and begin with our lessons. Bridie, will you hand out the slates and pencils, please?"

Oh… I have been so in awe of Dr Spicer and her handling of the children that I have quite forgotten something. In fact, I have clean forgotten to collect the box of slates from the general store since the doctor first mentioned it all that time ago.

"Sorry! I-I will run and fetch them now. I'll be quick!" I apologise, hurrying to fetch my shawl from a peg on the wall.

"That's all right, we can practise some spellings aloud in the meantime," says Dr Spicer.

"Wait, I'll help!" I hear Easter call out as she follows me outside, where feathery snowflakes are again beginning to flurry.

"Are you sure you want to come over to Mr Nathaniel's?" I ask her. "After what Charlie just said?"

"Met plenty like him," says Easter. "It hurts like hell but I'll be damned if I let him see that."

I don't usually like to hear cursing, but I think if anyone has earned a right to use words such as those, Easter has.

"I'm glad you came to school today," I tell her as we stand on the stoop, quickly fastening our shawls about us. "And I'm truly sorry if I seemed rude when you saw me last."

"And I'm sorry if I spoke sharply," says Easter. "But

Mrs Eriksson has no one to look out for her but me."

"So her husband…?"

"He can't abide her. He married himself a pretty young thing and is now embarrassed at her being poorly," Easter says with a despairing roll of her eyes.

"You know, when you caught me staring in the window, I was just surprised – I did not expect to catch sight of your mistress," I try to explain as we step on to the rucked and frozen road. "I imagined her to be asleep upstairs. You said she usually is in her bed during daylight?"

"Yes, but Mrs Eriksson didn't take her sleeping draught with her breakfast that morning since she knew the stamp mill would be quiet for Christmas," says Easter. "And she was enjoying hearing the music coming from the camp."

I am suddenly cheered to think of that lonely young woman taking some pleasure in the jigs and reels she heard played by Father and the others. Last time I suggested it, Easter had been very certain that her mistress would see no one. But maybe Mrs Eriksson is thawing a little…?

But that thought fades as I see Easter staring at me, as she has done before.

"What?" I say, as we take the uneven steps up to Nat's Store. "Why do you look at me so strangely?"

Why have you *always* looked at me so strangely when

we have talked before, I should have said.

"You ... you have eyes like the Indian's dog!" Easter exclaims, breaking out into a smile. "I've never seen eyes your colour in a person."

"Well, what a compliment – to be compared to a dog!" I joke in return.

And now Easter and I are both grinning broadly, delighted, I think, to find some unexpected fun in each other. In this moment she is not a respectful servant, and I am not a respectable teacher-in-training. We are young girls, and to be silly is as delicious as a lump of maple sugar melting on the tongue.

"But if my sisters were here, you would know *three* people with eyes this colour," I tell her. "We look nothing alike except for our eyes."

I think of the framed pencil drawing on the shelf in the parlour of Gillespie's store – of me sitting on the rock at the top of the towering Glas Crags, staring off to the horizon, to the west. Of course you cannot see the light grey of my eyes in that, but the colour of them was clear in the large oil-on-canvas version our artist friend Samuel painted in his studio at his and Caroline's apartments back in Glasgow. I wonder what has become of that painting of me now? Is it still with Samuel and Caroline and Ishbel, in London, where they planned to go soon after we parted at the docks in Scotland?

"And where are these sisters of yours?" asks Easter,

pausing on the stoop outside the door of the store.

"I don't know," I tell her truthfully. "They didn't want to come to America. But I have quite lost touch with them. And you...? Do you have family back in Chicago?"

"I have the pastor and his wife – they brought me up. They take in orphans," says Easter. "But once any of the children are grown, the pastor finds them positions and they move on, so—"

We both suddenly hold still at the sound of harsh, raised voices coming from inside the shop. I step towards the closest window and peer into the gloom.

"It's Mr Nathaniel and the mine manager... I can *just* see them in the back room," I whisper as I watch the two red-faced men raging at each other.

"Can you make out what they're saying?" Easter whispers back.

"Hold on," I say, then hover, putting my ear close to the glass, and catching a snippet or two. "Mr Eriksson is saying he shouldn't have listened to Mr Nathaniel... And now – *now* Mr Nathaniel is saying how *dare* Mr Eriksson say that when his plan is the best one for the mine and the town!"

"I bet Mr Nathaniel's plan will be best for *him*, whatever it is," murmurs Easter.

"True," I agree, before something strikes me and I turn to her. "Easter, won't you get into trouble from your master if he sees you here? Will he not insist you should be at home?"

"It's all right, he knows I'm attending school today," says Easter. "His wife told him she wanted me to learn to read and write so I can be of more use to her."

I can't help notice a smile twitch at the corner of Easter's mouth.

"What?" I hiss at her.

"She just said so because she knows I wanted to attend school and learn more. I can read and write fine – Pastor Jacob ran a school for the children of black folk at the back of the church. And I read books in the evening to Mrs Eriksson all the time, only *he* doesn't know that since he drinks so much wine he's always snoring in his armchair after dinner."

Ha! The mine manager must think himself the most important man in town, yet he is being fooled in his very own home. And I love to think Easter and her mistress are in cahoots. In their isolation and loneliness, it seems as if Mrs Eriksson and Easter have found more in common than the older husband and his young wife.

"If we go in quietly, they might not notice us, and we can find out what this mysterious plan is!" I say with a lift of my eyebrows as I gently push open the roughly planed wooden door.

But our high spirits are snuffed out as soon as we enter Nat's Store.

For the barrel of a shotgun is pointed straight at us.

"What're you two cackling about?" asks Charlie, his elbows on the desk, taking the weight of the gun.

"Put that away, you little fool!" roars Mr Nathaniel, storming out of the back room now he sees what his son is up to.

Behind him, a nervous-looking Mr Eriksson disappears further into the shadows of the back room, as if he hopes – foolishly – that Easter and I might not notice him.

"Ow!" yelps Charlie, wincing as his father slaps him around the head. "I was just protecting us! It could have been anyone ... a bear!"

"A *bear*? What kind of fool have I raised?" the storekeeper growls, grabbing the gun and placing it on a high shelf. "Now then, what is it you're wanting, missy?"

"I've heard you have here some packages of school slates and pencils," I say as confidently as I can.

"Well, you heard right," he replies, making no move to fetch the parcels from wherever they are stored, and making no move to recognise Easter's very existence.

As Mr Nathaniel talks, I study him. I see the scars of burns, the puckered folds of skin around his eye socket. They are pulled tight, sewn quickly and poorly. They *must* cause him constant pain. Father said we should be kind and thoughtful to all, in spite of their rank or demeanour. And I am thoughtful now, wondering if Mr Nathaniel once worked in the mines himself, before he traded a dark, dangerous life – one that possibly maimed him – for that of a storekeeper. And the pain he suffers must surely have helped make him the bitter man he is. That and the worry of being a merchant in a failing town with a failing copper mine. In fact, now that I remember, was it the uncertain future of the mine that Mr Nathaniel and Mr Eriksson were arguing about on Christmas Day? Might that be what they were heatedly talking of now? How to save the mine, the town and their livelihoods! Though quite how they mean to do it I cannot guess…

"Well, then," he says briskly, rousing me from my reverie. "Where is your money, missy!"

"Money?" I reply with a frown.

"Your doctor friend who is playing at schools – doesn't she realise that slates and pencils cost a pretty penny?"

Now I see red again and my sympathy fades away quicker than butter in a hot pan.

"Sir, I was told the mining company already bought and paid for those things!" I tell him sharply.

The storekeeper snorts, holding his arms up as if he has been caught.

"Ah, forgive me, my little vixen – I forgot."

And with that lie he wanders into the back room

and returns with two large brown-paper parcels tied with twine. He thuds them on the counter in front of us, causing a layer of dust to puff up from it. Just as I go to take the top parcel, Mr Nathaniel pulls both swiftly away.

"Now then, there is the matter of a fee for *storage* all these months," he says, curling his mouth in a wicked smile.

In that moment, something snaps inside me. Back on Tornish, I was a scared girl, frightened by the terrible power the new Laird and his family had over us all. And in Glasgow, I was petrified for my brother when the roguish older lads he thought friends *threatened* him into stealing for them. But I refuse to be scared any more. The Laird, his vindictive daughter Miss Kitty, the scoundrels Lachlan knew – we have left them behind in Scotland. We are as far, far away from them as can be. And I'll not let *anyone* bully me a minute longer.

"I'll thank you to give me that parcel, Mr Nathaniel, or I'll—"

BOOM!

A deep, bone-rattling sound.

An explosion that should not have happened, not so soon after the last one, not by a long way.

An explosion that makes the ground shake underfoot more than any other since we have been here.

We all pause, as the whole town does in the seconds

after a planned underground explosion in the mine tunnels. Always the pause is followed by a reassuring silence, and folk can quickly get back on with their work or cooking or mending, secure in the knowledge that all is well.

But this time, for the first time since I have been here, there is no minute of quiet calm. Shouts of panic are bellowed from the direction of the mine works.

And now a heavy brass bell clangs and clangs and *clangs* a mournful alarm.

"Lord, no... NO!" Mr Eriksson roars, appearing in the doorway to the back room, his hand clamped to his forehead.

As for Mr Nathaniel, he stands motionless, his jaw slack.

In this moment, what thoughts cross the minds of these grown men I cannot say. But even though I do not have their knowledge of a mining community, I can guess – be quite sure in fact – that some disaster has befallen the men below ground. A disaster that is not helped by standing still and gawping, as the storekeeper and mine manager are currently doing.

Throwing the door open, I bolt out of Nat's Store – Easter at my heels – at the same time as Dr Spicer bursts out of the Gillespie building across the street, Jean following right behind.

"Bridie, fetch my bag from my room and get Lachlan

and one of the boys to bring my trunk from my bedside to the mine head!" she orders.

Bunching her skirts up high, the doctor runs, as fast and with as much abandon as any man, in the direction all the townsfolk are now headed, just as a long, low screaming starts up…

CHAPTER 8

The crowd ahead is a blur, partly because it is a restlessly moving shape in the softly, steadily falling snow – more folk joining it, swelling it with every second.

And partly it is blurred because my hair has unravelled entirely as I run and it half blinds me. But with both my hands clutching Dr Spicer's heavy bag to my chest I can do little about it.

"Here, I'll take a handle," Easter offers, reaching towards the heavy bag I've been struggling to hold and run with, my weaker hand straining painfully with the weight of it.

Thankful for her help, I let her share the burden, and now with a handle each we quickly fall into a run together, footstep matching footstep.

"Bridie, Easter, over here!" Dr Spicer calls out to us, waving above the heads of the waiting and wailing women and children.

We both hurry all the more, breathless and hearts racing. I'm trusting that my brother and some other strong boy are somewhere behind us with the trunk containing the rest of Dr Spicer's medical things, but I'm more set on looking toward the doctor than looking over my shoulder.

"Excuse me, excuse me," I say, twisting this way and that through the crush, hearing Easter's voice right behind me, dovetailing *my* words with her own "Thank you, ma'am, thank you, sir..."

And now we are close to the entrance to the mine. The men from below ground have begun to emerge – coughing, dirt-covered, blood-streaked – to be greeted with gasps and a shrouding of snowflakes.

Those who were working up here on firm ground – rather than down in the dangerous depths – are quick to pull the unfortunate miners from the tunnel mouth, passing them back to a procession of waiting arms and the cold air their lungs must be gasping for. It is hard to tell one miner from the other in their strange uniform of disaster, but as Henni has thrown herself at a skinny young man, I guess it must be her brother Oskar, alive but clutching his hands to his chest, where a bloom of red spreads.

At the end of the procession of helpers I see my Father and Jean taking the weight of a badly injured lad. His leg hangs twisted and clearly broken, his jagged yells confirming the pain he feels.

They look to the newly arrived Mr Eriksson to see

where they might take the lad, but the mine manager stands rubbing his hands back and forth through his white-blond hair, as if he cannot comprehend what he is seeing, as if he cannot bear the load of a disaster on top of the worry of his failing business.

"Mr Eriksson, where shall we take the wounded? *Mr Eriksson!*" Dr Spicer shouts over to him, to no avail.

"This shouldn't have happened!" a florid-faced Mr Nathaniel calls out, lumbering to Mr Eriksson's side. "Was it *her*, d'you think? It has to be the Chippewa woman's curse come true, surely!"

"*Käften!*" Mr Eriksson snaps at him in Swedish, his face a matching red of panic. "You said nothing could go wrong! Does this seem like *nothing* to you?"

Realising that the mine manager seems too distracted – and about as much use as a swaddled babe to his men at the moment – I hurriedly make a suggestion to the doctor.

"Perhaps we could take them to the canteen?" I say, pointing over to the long, low wooden building close by.

"Yes … and the men could be lain out on the tables," says Dr Spicer, already on the move.

"And *we* can help," one of the waiting wives calls after her.

"Good," replies Dr Spicer, nodding vaguely in the women's direction as she quickly sizes up the cuts on the next man stumbling forth. "There are medical supplies in a cupboard in the building by the stamp mill. Can some of you go fetch what's there? Bandages and linseed oil for burns is what we need. And the rest of you, please find or tear up as many clean rags as you can spare in case we run out of bandages!"

The sound of distress ebbs as those watching and waiting find a sudden purpose.

"Now, Bridie," says Dr Spicer, talking to me over her shoulder as she waves those supporting the wounded to follow her. "*I* will assess the injured as they come into the canteen and ask some of the women to clean up the less badly hurt. But can you assist me? I'll need the strength of your father and Jean to hold down the lad with the broken leg while I put it back in place, but I'll need someone to pass me instruments or whatever I might require. Can you do that?"

All the difficult times in my life so far – they flicker quickly through my mind like flashes of lightning on a distant horizon. I have borne them all and I have borne them well. And as Dr Spicer herself told me, I can set my mind to anything I want to.

"Yes, I can," I tell her surely.

"And what can *I* do, ma'am?" asks Easter as Dr Spicer sets off towards the canteen and we hurry alongside her, our booted feet slipping in the ruts of frozen earth as we still hold tight to her medical bag.

"I suspect you are a decent needleworker, Easter," she says briskly, barely looking at the girl. "Is that correct?"

"Oh, yes, I am, ma'am," Easter answers. "And I sewed animal hide too, as the pastor let me try apprenticing with a shoemaker before I settled on maid's work. *And* I stitched a gash in the pastor's head once when he was roughed up by some white fellows that came by our church one time."

I shoot a look at Easter, wanting to know why such a shocking event should have happened – but there is no time to ask.

"Then I'll set you to stitching some of the wounds, Easter," Dr Spicer says plainly, as if she were asking the girl something as ordinary as darning a stocking.

The doctor suddenly stops for a second, as if it occurs to her what she's asking of girls as young as ourselves.

"I hope you both understand that it's not fair of me to ask these things of the miners' wives here – they might see their own husbands brought out broken, or dead, even. I need assistants who will hold themselves steady. Is that clear?" she says giving us both a steely stare.

Easter and I look at each other, then back at the doctor, nodding as hard as we can.

"Yes," we mutter, not quite in unison, but certainly as adamant as each other.

"Then, ladies, let us get to work…"

Several long hours later, Mr Nathaniel mutters a low oath as he walks into the canteen building.

He has come to collect the Irishman Seamus, the very last patient, and one of his lodgers at the store. Perhaps the storekeeper has sworn at the sorrowful sight of this bruised-faced fellow as he sits swaying on a bench, his head swaddled roughly in cloth that covers the newly stitched cut in his head.

Or perhaps Mr Nathaniel's foul-mouthed swear word was due to the sight of the long canteen table that Lachlan is trying his best to clean. Instead of crumbs and grease from the miners' meals, it is sweat and blood that my brother wipes away with any wretched rags he can lay his hands on.

Then again, perhaps the man is taken aback by the sight of Dr Spicer, Easter and myself standing dirtied and wild-eyed at our posts as if we have staggered from a battlefield. I suspect we might look a little mad, but the truth of it is, our eyes sparkle with relief, with happiness.

For no one died today. By some miracle, no wife was widowed and no child ended up fatherless. The explosion-gone-wrong in the mine tunnel… The worst of it was the young Cornishman with the badly broken leg, an older German fellow with a terrible, deep gash to his stomach, and Henni's big brother Oskar who lost all the fingers of one hand, blown clean off in the blast. As for the rest, there were countless burns, grazes and wounds that needed cleaning and treating and stitching, and men with chests that were tight and sore from their panicked time in the smoke-choked tunnels below.

But as the winter's afternoon light began to dim, as we fixed up Seamus here, as the stream of patients finally dwindled and men were helped away home to their beds in the cabins and lodgings … it felt as if we had won some war. We three, aided by the army of wives and children that washed and cleaned and bandaged and cared, along with the men that carried and consoled and held their fellow men.

The giddying sensation of it swells in my chest, and I am not quite sure what to do with it.

"Seamus will be fine," I hear Dr Spicer tell the storekeeper. "He might be dizzy and confused awhile but should be better with a decent sleep."

"Aye, *I'll* be fine," mutters the miner, rousing now at the mention of his name. "But will *you* be fine, Mr Nathaniel? Will you?"

The storekeeper's face darkens as he pulls his lodger to his feet.

"Gently, Mr Nathaniel!" Dr Spicer urges him.

He throws her a filthy look in return and grips the now-standing Seamus under one arm.

"C'mon, man," he orders him forward.

Seamus tries to pull away, roaring, "How's your conscience, eh?"

"And how'd you like all the rum you can drink when we get back to the store, for free, eh?" Mr Nathaniel counters, holding Seamus all the tighter and steering the staggering miner towards the canteen door.

"What does the Irishman mean?" Easter wonders aloud.

"I heard some of the women saying that Mr Nathaniel's been holed up in the mine-manager's office most of the day," says Lachlan, passing us by with a bucket half filled with rags and water stained red on his way out for fresh water. "Suppose it's made folk angry, seeing both of them in there instead of out helping."

"Speaking of Mr Eriksson, I think I'll have a word with him about the care his workers will need after this. We have woefully few medical supplies left..." Dr Spicer mutters, heading off after the men.

And with that, Easter and I are the only two left in this echoingly empty room. Like a puppet with its strings cut, I collapse down on to a bench.

"Think folks'll see her as a *real* doctor now?" says Easter, flopping herself next to me.

"I hope so," I answer.

Though in this moment, I am thinking of Easter rather than Dr Spicer; she has had more to bear today, having to face men who were frightened and in pain yet railed against a dark-skinned young girl stitching their wounds. But help them she did as wives shushed and begged the injured to be still and let her help them, in the same way as other wives begged *their* loved ones and friends to let Dr Spicer – assisted by a girl such as myself – make them better.

"To think she'll have slept all through this strange day..." Easter says thoughtfully.

At first, my exhausted mind struggles to understand who exactly Easter refers to. For a moment, I fancy that she talks of the mystical, night-wandering Indian maiden; there's been enough gloomy talk of the "Chippewa Curse" amongst folk in here today, though Dr Spicer – with her scientific leaning – has quickly and forcefully shushed any such nonsense in her hearing.

"Your mistress, you mean?" I ask Easter once my thoughts clear. "You think Mrs Eriksson will not have woken with the noise and the shouting?"

Easter shakes her head. "She takes such a strong dose of her medicine every morning that she'd sleep through a *volcano* erupting, I reckon. It's her escape from this place – this prison, she calls it."

"So she is very unhappy here?" I ask Easter, understanding how this far-flung place could drive a person half mad, especially with the dreadful heartbeat of the stamp mill clanging day in and day out.

"She got wed in a terrible hurry in London, thinking she'd have a fine old time as a married lady in America. She reckoned she'd be living in Chicago, as Mr Eriksson promised, taking tea and promenading with society ladies like herself," Easter explains, holding her chin high, mimicking the ways of rich women. "Instead, her husband drags her here to Hawk's Point, where there is nothing for her to do and *more* than plenty of time to do nothing in…"

"Can she not leave him? Go back to her family?" I suggest, imagining – with more than a little envy – Mrs Eriksson heading away on the first steamship of the spring.

"There's the trouble – she's got nowhere to go," says Easter. "Her pa is dead, and gambled most of the family money away, she told me. Her mama doesn't want to know about her troubles. She even wrote and told Mrs Eriksson that leaving her husband would be too shameful, and that she would just have to make the best of it."

What a heartless thing for a mother to say. Many a time I heard Mother say the Gaelic phrase "*an rud nach gabh leasachadh, 's fheudar cur suas leis*" (what cannot be cured must be endured), but I cannot imagine her ever letting one of her girls suffer in a miserable marriage.

"How old do you think your mistress is?" I ask.

"Maybe nineteen, maybe twenty," Easter guesses as she spins.

Nineteen or twenty! Younger than I imagined and only a few years older than myself; nearer the ages of my beloved Effie and Ishbel, I think. How sad to be so alone and without family, for all the comforts that Mrs Eriksson might have.

"Your mistress's situation – it puts me in mind of someone I used to know," I tell Easter. "A young woman came to our island in Scotland. Caroline was distant kin of the Laird who owned the place. She might have seemed like another rich lady to any stranger, but in truth, she was almost a prisoner, unwanted and uncared for."

"What happened to her?" asks Easter.

"My family had to leave the island as fast as we could, once we heard that the Laird thought Father was plotting against him. And so my sisters and I … we decided to smuggle Caroline away with us, from under her guardian's very nose!"

I give a little shiver, recalling that frightening time and the risks we took. But how could we have abandoned a young woman when she had no one who truly cared for her but us?

Oh, how the Laird must have hated us! Especially as we stole away his dog Patch too… It was plain that he didn't have a warm thought for either his poorly neglected ward or the pet he'd happily kick and beat, but a man like that would resent the dent to his pride.

"Is that so? That's like Pastor Jacob!" Easter says with eyes wide. "We often had folk staying with us for just a short time. Took me till I was near grown to understand they were slaves on the run from the southern states, and the pastor's home and church was a stopping point for them on their way north to Canada. Didn't realise how dangerous it was till some bounty-hunter fellows came looking for runaways, and beat up the pastor when they didn't find them."

"Was that the time you stitched his head?" I check, making sense of what she said earlier.

"Yes…" she says, nodding thoughtfully at that unsettling memory. "But you know, *some* folk that stopped by were free black people from eastern cities, heading to homestead in the west. They'd come by train and stay awhile till they bought themselves wagons and horses and supplies for their journeying. There was this real nice lady – Mrs Clarice Campbell, her name was. She sent me a letter before I left Chicago, saying she and her husband had found themselves a homestead near a little town in Minnesota. Hopetown it was called, something pretty like that. Think I might like to go out that way once I saved myself enough money."

"Really?" I ask, knowing I must look goggle-eyed with surprise. "I've always had a yearning to go west too!"

"Well, let's go together!" Easter says lightly, holding a bloodied hand out to shake mine.

"Yes, let's!" I say, beaming at the idea of someone sharing my dreams when I know not *one* other person who does.

But even with my spirit soaring and my own bloodied hand very definitely shaking on our agreement, I know in my heart of hearts it cannot happen.

For Father's days of running are over. From the island to Glasgow, from Glasgow to New York, from New York to Hawk's Point... He would not see fit to move on again, I'm sure. Not unless something *drove* us from this place, as it did everywhere else.

But surely our days of ill-luck are over...?

CHAPTER 9

Ever since the mine disaster, the weather has sulked, throwing us blinding snowstorms and terrible winds that toyed with the trees, tossing them around as if they were playthings.

But today is different. The air is still, the sky is bright blue, and the children of the Gillespie storefront classroom are quite daft, infected by the lightness, giddy at the glimpse of finer days to come even though it is still only March.

"In Scots Gaelic, we call it *Am Màrt*," I tell the children, as Dr Spicer marks their writing at her desk.

"*Am Màrt*," the children roar their sing-song response, just as they did when the Irish boys bellowed "*Mí Márta*", and Henni and Matilde trilled "*März!*" in perfect unison in their clipped German accents.

But the Chippewas have far and away the best name for this month, as the pupils are about to find out.

"Jean, can you tell us what your word is?" I ask him.

"My people know this time as Snow Crust Moon.

LITTLE BIRD LANDS

Naabidin is snow crust, *Giizis* means moon," says Jean from his stool in the corner where his fingers deftly work on some colourful band or belt.

Wampum this craft is called. Jean has tried to teach me how to do it on those evenings he sometimes comes to share a meal with my family and Dr Spicer. Sadly, my fingers are clumsy and I spill more beads than I stitch; Odayan always watches with curiosity as they trickle between the cracks in the floorboards. I stumble too when I try to say the words of Jean's language, but still I try. And in these long winter nights, when the wind howls and moans and rattles the thin clapboard walls, often all that helps lull me to sleep in the biting cold is to murmur the names of the months of the year over and over again, first in Chippewa and then in English: Spirit Moon, Bear Moon, Snow Crust Moon, Sugar Moon, Sucker Moon, Blossom Moon, Berry Moon, Ricing Moon, Changing Leaves Moon, Falling Leaves Moon, Freezing Moon, Little Spirit Moon…

"Can you say it again, please, Jean?" I ask.

"*Naabidin Giizis,*" he replies.

Somewhere under a table I can hear the happy whack of his dog's tail on the floor. Perhaps Odayan enjoys hearing his master's voice, but I think it more likely that he has placed himself at Lachlan's feet as usual and has just been fed a scrap my brother has saved from our breakfast table. Nearly all the children are in awe of

Odayan, wishing they had such a creature themselves, but it is my brother who he softens for.

"*Naabidin Giizis*," the children repeat excitedly, enjoying the taste of these different-sounding words in their mouths.

All except Charlie that is. He came crawling back to school a few weeks ago, once he realised how dull it was to be on his own. He now pulls a face as if he has been asked to eat something sour and unpleasant. His eyes are lowered, fidgeting with a piece of string, I notice.

"Very nice pronunciation!" says Dr Spicer getting up from her chair. "And that –" she takes a look at the clock, whose thin, metal hands finally reach up together in prayer, pointing straight at twelve – "brings us to the end of school for today. Do *not* rush, and *no* pushing and shoving as you leave…"

But Dr Spicer is guilty of doing all three as she belts herself into her oversized coat and squeezes past the chattering children before they have barely put their mittens and mufflers on. I understand her haste; today is her first appointment with the mine manager's wife, which is why Easter leaves with her. It is fair to say that the trust and respect shown to Dr Spicer in the aftermath of the mine-tunnel collapse has made her the busiest person in town, with her swelling roll call of pupils to deal with in the mornings, and the surgeries she holds in the same storefront in the afternoons. All the hard work seems to suit Dr Spicer though. I recall her being gaunt and pale when we first met back in November (the month of the Freezing Moon!) But she is more than a little changed: pink-cheeked, a little plumper perhaps, but bonny.

Now, with the doctor already gone, I take her place by the door while the children chat and jostle their way out. As I say my goodbyes, I hear Odayan give a low warning growl and look round to see Charlie at the end of the line, turning back into the room, holding the string he was fidgeting with.

A flush of anger floods my face for I see he has made a slingshot of it! He seems about to ready his aim, about to let go of one end of the string so that some small, sharp stone will fly in the direction of the still-seated Jean, when Odayan's growl turns to a menacing bark. Fear makes Charlie hesitate long enough for me to snatch the slingshot from his hand.

"Hey!" he calls out. "Give that back!"

"Get out," I say firmly. "I'll be telling Dr Spicer about this."

"Well, tell her about that dangerous dog, then!" he blusters, pointing to Odayan, who now stands silent, at Jean's command.

But for all his cocky words, Charlie moves fast enough, hurrying out of the doorway and away down the steps. I slam the door shut and lean against it, tossing the hateful slingshot on a nearby table.

"I'm sorry about that," I say to Jean.

"What are you sorry for? It's not *your* weapon," he replies, slowly wrapping up his beadwork and placing it into his satchel. At his feet, Odayan relaxes and yawns, long, white fangs glinting. "The boy and some of the others in town have got braver with what they say to me since the mine accident."

He's right; I'm saddened to say that sense has quite left the townspeople. With no explanation for the disastrous second explosion, with worry about the future of the mine, with no chance of copper being found while they dig out and shore up the collapsed tunnel, folk have been looking for someone to blame. Rumours have taken hold, superstition has won out. It *had* to be the work of the Chippewa Curse and the black-feathered ghost they say. And if they cannot properly rage at a spectre, then they choose the next best thing and rage at a real living Indian. Even one who helped as much as anyone on the day of the disaster.

"You could just tell them that the spirit doesn't exist," I suggest.

"They never took my word on anything before, so they won't now they've worked themselves up into a fever," says Jean, putting on his hat and heading for the door, Odayan falling in step. "Think it's maybe time

I got out of Hawk's Point for a while. Going to fix up my sled and go overland to visit my family on the reservation."

"No!" I say, shocked. "We'd all miss you too much!"

And Lachlan would be devastated to say goodbye to Odayan, I think to myself.

"Huh," is all Jean says in reply, as he takes his leave.

I lean in the doorway and watch him walk away without a backward glance, though he raises a hand to me over his shoulder. At his side, Odayan matches his master's long, loping walk with a hunch-shouldered bounce of his own. They leave the road and wend between the buildings further along, heading up into the snowy woods and the cabin they both share somewhere in the foothills of the forested cliff.

I'm about to go inside when I see Easter hurrying back along the road.

"Is everything all right?" I ask, stepping down to meet her.

"I told Dr Spicer I heard some of the children talking about a pond in the woods where you can slide and skate," she says, struggling for breath. "Heard them say it's not far, just up behind the town. Dr Spicer asked if you and me could go on up there together and hustle any children we find back down to their mothers…"

"I *knew* they were all too giddy today," I say in reply, grabbing my shawl from a hook by the door. "At least the snow will make it easier to track them."

In just a few moments, Easter and I are following in the frosted footsteps of the children, heading uphill into the light-dappled trees at the foot of the cliff.

Holding our skirts high, their hems already soaked heavy, Easter and I both pant with the effort. And with those chest-pumping breaths, a subtle, sweet perfume suddenly comes to me, making me quite giddy myself. There's a scent in the air; the nuttiness of the pines, a soft wind that is no longer full of sharp ice to freeze the lungs. I smell loosening buds on branches and pinpricks of green shoots that unfurl in patches where the snow is beginning to melt.

The scent is of change, spring, hope.

Raising my face to the blue sky above the treetops, I can almost feel the gentle rhythmic pounding of birds' wings in the sky above as they begin to drift northward in their vee formations, turning their feathered backs on southern wintering spots to return to their Michigan homelands.

And talking of birds, I see a gleaming black crow's feather on a mossed tree trunk and gather it up to add to my brother's collection, cheerfully sticking it in my hair as I set off again.

I'm about to take a high step forward over the stump when the back of Easter's hand gently presses against my chest, and I stop in my tracks to see what *she* sees.

Ah, we are being watched! A few feet away from us is a deer – a hind with amber eyes and the steam of her breath haloing at her wet, dark nose.

I expect the dainty animal to instantly leap away. When she does not, when she stays exactly where she is, with no fear, I have a thought; I am filled with a sudden sense that perhaps *Mother* is trying to reach out and tell me something. Trying to let me know that the snowed-in prison of Hawk's Point is beginning to loosen its shackles. Back down at the waterfront, the ice that clings tight to edges of the vast Lake Superior will be already thinning, I realise, ready to let the first steamship come through in a few weeks' time. Fresh supplies, new people and packets of mail will come (though I try not to think of those last, precious items). This steep forest that has seemed like a frozen bear trap around the town; it can now begin to start showing its beauty, its bounty, its rough but soon recognisable paths that will lead to other settlements just a few miles along the coast either side.

Maybe – despite the mood in the town right now – this place *might* begin to feel properly like home to me?

"...*WHAT shall we do with the DRUNKEN sailor!*"

The loudly sung words break the spell, and the hind – this wonder of nature more miraculous than some poor creature on show in Barnum's American

Museum – is gone in a near-silent bound.

And behind where she stood, I see now something glittering, shining through the bars of great, gnarled tree trunks.

"Look!" says Easter, spotting it too.

A few root-tripping steps further and we come to an open space, the length and breadth of it made up of a pond, frozen hard and marled white.

The three girls on the ice – Henni, Matilde and Morwen – cannot hear us above the glory of their shouted song, a cheeky sea shanty learned from the Irish lads.

"...WHAT shall we do with the DRUNKEN sailor!" Easter joins in, running on to the ice and sliding into a spin on her smooth-soled black boots.

As the girls squeal in surprise and delight, Easter's arms windmill around her, her ragged shawl spiralling out behind like a solitary woollen wing as she skates. I am about to applaud her when – with a sudden wobble and clatter – Easter's boots go quick-quick from under her and she is sprawled flat out, laughter crippling her so much she cannot raise herself up.

I take hurried but small tip-tapping steps across the ice to help, but Henni and the other girls are already getting Easter to her feet. At that moment I remember our purpose.

"What are you doing here?" I ask the girls, wiping

back my hair now that it has wriggled its way free from its pins and tumbles to my waist. "The ice might not be safe, there could be wild animals, or you might step in a trap!"

"It's all right – we're not alone," says Morwen. "The others are here somewhere. We could call for help."

It's a poor excuse for sense. Speaking of that, where is my brother?

"Did Lachlan come up to the woods?" I ask, guessing that he would find it hard to resist any fun to be had if everyone else was joining in.

"Yes, the rest of them went exploring that way," says Matilde, pointing towards a high-ridged bank on the far side of the pond.

I listen for the sound of capering and I hear nothing – but I *see* something. That bank... In it is a large dip with scrubby low bushes in its lap. Above it, a thick crust of snow – *naabidin* – pushes over the edge of the ridge.

It is the strangest thing; I have never been to this place before and yet the *shape* of what I see before me is somehow very familiar.

"What's wrong?" asks Easter, noticing that my attention has been stolen away.

"I think... I think I *know* what this place is!" I tell her, my heart beating a rhythm of excitement as I walk towards the bank.

The others follow, wondering what I find so fascinating.

"Look," I say, drawing a shape with my finger. "Does it not mimic the entrance to the mine head back in the settlement?"

"What do you mean?" says Easter, her tone uncertain as she stares at the dipped wall of earth under the awning of the ridge.

"Jean told me there was copper aplenty in the mountains if you knew where to look," I say, staring at the possible shape of an original opening. "The Chippewa have legends of long-lost mines worked by ancient peoples."

"Ooh, look! So pretty!" coos Henni, pointing down at the pond's edge.

We all bend and peer, spotting tiny glinting red-gold pebbles caught in the ice.

"Copper?" suggests Easter, turning to look at me questioningly.

"I think so..."

"You know what this means?" says Easter.

"That we might have found a mine?" I laugh.

"More than that! You might have *saved* the town," Easter replies, her pretty eyes wide.

"Oh, does this mean we can stay and not have to move somewhere else again?" asks Matilde as Morwen jumps up and down, clapping her mittened hands and squealing.

"Maybe this will cheer my papa!" Henni suggests. "He is in such a dark temper all the time, especially with my brother."

I look at the desperately hopeful faces of the younger girls and wonder if this truly is something that will lift the black mood that has hung over Hawk's Point like a stubborn sea mist these last weeks.

But wait…

"Why is your father angry with Oskar?" I ask Henni, thinking that *sympathy* for the poor lad is more in order after the injury he sustained in the explosion.

"He is angry because my brother plays cards for money all the time. Father disapproves of—"

BANG!

We all halt as a sharp, too-close-for-comfort blast of gunshot rings out.

"Hunters?" says Easter, clutching the three smaller girls about her, feeling like myself, all of a sudden so very far from safety.

Dread crushes my chest and my legs threaten to crumple beneath me as I think of the beautiful hind…

Then a terrible yowling commences, followed by desperate shouts. A hunter would not call out like that, I am certain. I am also certain that no hunter would sound so young.

"No, no, NO!" the voice yelps.

My *brother's* voice.

"Lachlan! LACHLAN!" I shout back, cupping my hands to my mouth so that my voice might reach him wherever he may be in this puzzle of endless trees.

But then there is a sudden crashing sound above us and our eyes are momentarily filled with falling snow from the ridge's edge. A shadow hurtles overhead, and a terrible whack, crack and whimper resounds from the hard surface of the pond behind us.

Easter, the three girls and I, we turn as one, shaking ourselves clear of our icy blinkers.

"Help! Help!" Charlie Nathaniel calls out, clutching a strangely twisted ankle with one hand, while a rifle – the one I saw him point at Easter and myself in his father's store on the day of the mining disaster – goes spinning and spiralling off across the ice.

But it is not the ankle Charlie has probably broken from his foolish and frankly dangerous leap that concerns me – it is the continuing snapping of the ice, water already rushing to the surface around him.

And it is as if that icy water suddenly flows in my veins. Easter and I are both quite small and thin, but if we two run together to Charlie's rescue, we will surely *all* be tipping into the breath-crushingly cold depths. But whatever has happened, however much I cannot bring myself to like the boy, I can hardly stand by and watch as the ice slowly gives way and he drowns, can I?

"Get away!" I order the now-sobbing younger girls, pointing to the safety of solid ground beyond the pond.

"Here!" Easter calls out and I see that she has run to a spindly, leafless tree that grows close to the frozen water's edge. I go to help her, and together we yank and tear off a branch in seconds.

"If I lie flat to spread my weight, I can reach him..." she says.

"I'm littler than you, and lighter," I remind Easter, as Charlie snivels and begs from the crackling, sinking middle of the ice. "*I'll* do it. Hold on to my skirts."

And so I flatten myself and crawl out as far as I dare, trying not to see the whirling waters that are seeping through the growing crevices.

"Grab it!" I order Charlie, as I throw the branch to him.

He feebly lunges, wild-eyed and sobbing, but manages at last to catch hold of it. I try to wriggle myself backwards on the ice, helped by a crouching Easter who tugs hard at my ankles and skirts. But I have miscalculated; yes, I might well be smaller than Easter, but she has two strong hands while I have only one that can *truly* grip hard and fast.

"Use your feet, Charlie! Push yourself towards me!" I shout again, feeling a panic set in as an ever-growing spiders' web of cracks spread from under Charlie's body.

He seems to try while I wriggle frantically backwards, Easter grunting and panting as she struggles to pull the combined weight of us. But truth be told, I do not know if this will work. I can hear and feel the cloth of my woollen skirt tearing where Easter pulls desperately at it, and I do not know that we can pull Charlie free in time, before both he and I join the rifle I have just seen tilt, slip and disappear beneath the surface with a death-like gurgle.

I only *just* hear Easter's sudden cry of surprise before I feel two large hands encircle my waist, crushing the air from my body but yanking myself — and in turn the branch and the snivelling boy — backwards to the safety of the pond's edge in one, two, *three* hard pulls.

"Jean!" I croak breathlessly, swivelling around to see my *Anishinaabe* friend get a hold of Charlie's coat and pull the injured boy clear, before roughly letting go of him and watching him flop to the slushy ground.

Jean says nothing but stands panting and wild-eyed himself.

And then I hear sobbing coming — peculiarly — from somewhere else entirely, from somewhere on high.

Blinking as fast and hard as my heart races, I glance upwards. On top of the ridge above us stands my brother, unsteady on his feet as he holds the heavy, flopping weight of Odayan in his arms. Great drops of red stain what remains of the snow crust. The dog's head lolls lifelessly, its grey eyes staring down, blind to the scene in front of it.

The hope, the joy I felt only minutes ago melts faster than snowflakes on a burning hot griddle...

CHAPTER 10

I cannot think what we must look like, this raggle-taggle band of children I lead out of the woods.

"*Ach du meine Güte!*" one of the German women calls out in alarm, dropping her gathered armfuls of kindling in the road at the sight of us.

The woman's panic pricks through my haze of sadness. For what must she think, seeing me come walking into town, all muddied and soaked, my shirt and skirt torn, propping up my brother who appears half murdered, his clothes and whole self so soaked in blood. Alongside us, Easter looks after the desperately sobbing Henni, Matilde and Morwen, while more of the boys and girls who'd happily scampered up into the woods now forlornly follow us out, after they heard the shot and yells and came scurrying to see what terrible thing had occurred.

As for Charlie, two of the Irish boys have an arm each and are – roughly, I think – helping him limp away from the terrible trouble he caused.

LITTLE BIRD LANDS

"Bridie! BRIDIE!" I hear Father call out as he runs from the school building he is near completing. "What has happened! Lachlan ... where are you injured?"

Lachlan can barely breathe from the crying, never mind answer Father's question.

"He is not injured," I quickly assure Father, as he holds my brother by the shoulders and looks him up and down. "Charlie stole a rifle from the general store. He killed Odayan."

"I thought it was a wolf!" Charlie protests somewhere behind me.

But I am done with that boy. I don't care for his excuses. All I know is that I will never forget the look on Jean's face as he walked back up the bank after saving Charlie, and wordlessly took the weight of his dead dog's body from my staggering brother.

"Go!" he'd roared, walking away from us. "Go – all of you! NOW!"

In that moment I knew Jean would leave Hawk's Point for certain and we'd never see him again.

"So none of you are hurt?" Father checks, casting his eyes over everyone while more folk appear, wondering what the commotion is about.

"Only Charlie – he's broke his ankle, I think," says Easter.

"You should go fetch Dr Spicer then, my dear," Father suggests to her, and I watch as my friend gently lets go of the younger girls, leaving them in the care of the womenfolk, before hurrying away towards the mine manager's house.

A surge of people now run and circle us, jabbering questions at us all.

"There's something else – Bridie found something!" I hear Henni pipe up as she finds herself being wrapped in the thick comfort of a woman's shawl.

But no one pays her any attention beyond making her cosy, or understands her meaning in the muddle of the moment.

"Bridie found something *important!*" she tries again, sounding frustrated, wrestling herself out of her knitted cocoon. "She found copper!"

The babble of voices eases.

And then begins again as everyone turns to me…

Several hours later, my ears are still ringing, from the loudness of the shot, from the awful cracking of the ice, from the incessant questioning, from the cries of excitement that reverberated up and down the settlement all day.

"So it looks like there really *might* be some copper to be found there?" asks Dr Spicer, holding Father's hands over the table in the parlour so she can inspect his grazed knuckles.

The team of men who went up to inspect the site

at the pond this afternoon had worked hard, clattering their pickaxes into bone-hard ground, digging with their shovels, sometimes clearing a few feet of earth with bare hands in their excitement.

"Aye, it seems promising," says Father, wincing a little as Dr Spicer dabs his raw skin with some potion of hers. "Where's Lachlan?"

"He's in the back bedroom," I reply.

After we got him home and cleaned him up, Lachlan took to his bed and lay silent and shivering, and would not be consoled. Eventually he cried himself to sleep – I laid another thick blanket over him when I went to check him a little while ago, before Father returned. He does not yet know that Father went to Jean's cabin this afternoon and found it empty and shut up, Jean long gone.

Myself, I've not been able to settle to anything. I washed and scrubbed our bloodied and dirtied clothes and hung them to freeze-dry on the rope at the back of the building. I made a stew for Father when he returned. I went back and forth to see to Lachlan. And all that done, I am not sure what to do with my restlessness.

"How was your patient today?" I hear Father ask, and realise I had forgotten about Dr Spicer meeting with the mine manager's young wife this afternoon.

"She is very low in spirits," the doctor replies. "And being isolated for so many months, she is bothered with her nerves when it comes to meeting new people. It will take a long time to gain her trust, I think, but she has agreed for me to visit her weekly. And she did listen when I told her how dangerous it is to take the sleeping tincture as much as she does, and has promised to use less of it and give it up eventually."

"Poor lass," says Father.

"Most of all, it is my opinion that she mustn't stay shut up in that house. I have looked out a pamphlet for her about the benefits of fresh air and exercise, even though the muscles in her legs will be weak from lack of use at the moment," says Dr Spicer, nodding at a folded sheet of paper on the table. "I'll give it to Easter in school tomorrow."

"Or I can deliver it now?" I suggest, seeing a way to walk off my fidgeting.

"Well, I suppose it is not *too* late," says Father, looking at the clock on the shelf, where the hour reads near seven.

"I won't disturb Mrs Eriksson," I assure the doctor, already reaching for my heavy jacket. "I'll just tap at the kitchen door for Easter."

With the pamphlet in my hand, I let myself out. Though the sky is dark, the Snow Crust Moon is full, and with its company of stars it will not be hard to find my way along the road. And another glow lights up the start of my short journey; Nat's Store is bright with lamplight and candles, loud with the voices of men inside, full of hope and ale.

I stop for a moment and watch the silhouetted heads at the windows, thinking of the miners smacking their tankards together in celebration, perhaps toasting *me* when they should be toasting Jean. For if *he* had not told me what to look for, I would never have spotted the old mine entrance. But no one wanted to hear that earlier, and I don't suppose they'll want to hear it now, or later either…

"Well, you *certainly* got them out of a fix, didn't you, Bridie?"

I halt at the sound of the voice, and at the sight of a hunched figure sitting in the shadows of the stoop.

"Seamus?" I say, recognising the lilt in the words spoken, though they might as well have been said in Hebrew for all the understanding I have of them.

Mr Nathaniel's lodger shuffles forward so that I might see him a little better in the pool of light from the nearest window. He clutches a sloshing tankard in his hand and seems unsteady. I swear Seamus has aged in the last few weeks; I'm not sure if it is due to dread of going down the mine each day after the accident, or the sheer amount of alcohol he has been drinking lately.

"See, the pair of them weren't sure they'd get away with it. But what *you* found today, it's got them out of trouble. And they don't deserve that…"

I can think of no answer for Seamus because I can't think what he means.

"You know, I said no to 'em, Bridie. Turned 'em down flat."

"Listen, I think I had better go," I mumble, pointing away along the road. But Seamus doesn't appear to hear me, so lost is he in his conversation with himself.

"That poor young boy. Didn't deserve to get hurt so bad…"

Wait – now he talks of Charlie? I cannot keep up. Luckily I am saved by Mr Nathaniel of all people.

"Ah, there you are, Seamus!" says the storekeeper, barging out of the door and giving me just the most cursory of glances. "Shall we get you in out of the cold? Maybe get you a shot of rum to warm you up, eh?"

Seeing my chance to leave, I slip away along the road, hurrying now that the evening temperature dips ever lower and the cold truly bites. More lights glow from small, square windows as I reach the miners' cabins, where I hear the clatter of domestic life inside the little houses: a lullaby sung here, a baby's cry there.

A minute more and I find myself at the winding path through the trees that leads to the mine manager's house. It's here that a little of my confidence begins to ebb, for the leafy canopy above shuts out the moon and starlight, pitching the path into darkness. Taking a deep breath, I push ahead, keeping my eyes on the faint glimmer of a gas lamp from the parlour.

"What's to fear?" I whisper to myself. "The worst things I have seen have come in the daylight. What terrors can the night hold?"

My stirring words work. For a whole few seconds that is – till I hear a sound.

A small sound, a barely there sound to the right of me, in the huddle of the pine trees: a crack of a stick, stepped on.

I freeze, my heart and my breathing held coil-tight in my chest. Have I been foolish to walk this way alone, thinking myself safe so close to the town? How can it not have occurred to me that while we are contained behind our walls, by our cosy stoves, the wolves might think to pad down from their hillside lairs to sniff curiously around our very doorsteps, no matter *how* early the hour of the evening?

As the blood suddenly races once again in my veins, I quickly turn to run back the way I came, to the road, to the fluttering hope of light from the nearby miners' cabins. But at that very second, the creature that lurks in the woods … it shows its shadowy shape to me, and I gasp with what little breath I can muster.

For it is no wolf.

It stands upright, looking my way. A full, dark cape, a hood, a slim, tall figure. Can it truly be *her*, the spectre, the curse-maker? But how can I see something that Jean himself confessed does not exist? Yet there she stands…

Whatever this person is, I see with a start that she has begun to turn and hurry from me as much as I was hurrying from her. Frightened footsteps crackle more sticks in her path.

And now it appears that she is not alone, this disappearing figure in the trees. A smaller shadow runs behind her, pulling free her long, heavy cape – made of *fur*, not feathers, I think – as it snags on branches.

Back in Scotland, these two might have been considered a pair of shape-shifting selkies. And no doubt the German and Cornish and Irish and Swedish folk in Hawk's Point have similar dark creatures they may call upon if they saw such figures in the woods.

But all of a sudden, I am certain that I can guess the true identity of the Chippewa ghost. She is one who drinks her secret sleeping potions like a princess from a folk tale, dreaming her way through the noise of the working day, only to rise in the quick of the night and drift like a phantom through the town, sometimes, just *sometimes*, glimpsed by one or other of the townsfolk.

She is someone who has no need of the pamphlet I carry, encouraging exercise and fresh air, since she sees to that already, in her own, secretive way.

She is Easter's mistress if I am not very much mistaken.

She is the mysterious, never-seen Mrs Eriksson.

LITTLE BIRD LANDS

And Easter is by her side.

Now they are a little closer to the glow of lamplight seeping from the window, I see Easter turn to me, raising a finger to her lips…

CHAPTER 11

Easter kept the secret of her mistress's after-dark wanderings very well all these last months.

And since stumbling upon it, I have *not*, I'm ashamed to say.

But then I've only shared it with the two people I trust most of all – Father and Dr Spicer. Father, since he is kind and decent and pities young Mrs Eriksson, although he has never had the pleasure of meeting her; Dr Spicer, since she is Mrs Eriksson's physician.

Much as I love my younger brother, I did not trust Lachlan with the secret. I worried that he might tell it without thinking, setting off a great rolling stone of gossip before he realised his mistake.

But most excitingly, this evening, I – along with Father and Lachlan – will finally meet the mysterious Mrs Eriksson face-to-face! It has been two weeks or so since I came across the entrance to the ancient mine works, and tonight there is to be a celebration at the Erikssons' house with – and I can hardly believe this

– myself as guest of honour. I have not seen them yet, but two important men from the mining company offices arrived here today, after travelling overland by dogs and sled, to witness for themselves this treasure chest of a find. Not only does the old mine contain great tracts of ore, but even a six-foot high boulder of pure copper, a thing so remarkable that it will make Hawk's Point famous across all of America, Mr Eriksson has proclaimed. Lachlan wonders if Mr P. T. Barnum himself might seek such a thing out for his museum!

"*Tha thu a 'coimhead brèagha*, Bridie!" Father compliments me now, as he runs his hands over his newly trimmed red beard.

"You're looking very handsome yourself," I answer him brightly.

It might just be the lamplight, but Father's eyes appear to glisten as he gazes upon me. I think it is not so much that I am all of a sudden "beautiful", it is more that I remind him a little of my eldest sister Ishbel tonight, with the tight black circlets of hair that Dr Spicer has neatly braided and pinned up for me. Not that they will stay neat for long, since my unruly hair tends to do what it pleases.

"You do look very lovely, my dear," Dr Spicer announces as she straightens the brooch at my neck that I have borrowed from her. It is made of jet and shows two hands holding a wreath. She had several brooches

I could have chosen; an oval of ruby-coloured paste gems, one of a bright painted sprig of flowers, a dove-blue cameo and more, but I chose this one, not just because the colour of the dark stone matched my hair, but because it is a mourning brooch which Dr Spicer wore after her husband died in the riding accident a few months back.

I dare say some at the gathering tonight might find it a peculiar choice of ornament, but they'll no doubt think it impolite to ask the reason why. I expect that the important men from the mining company would simply laugh if they knew it was in memory of a *dog* that was killed, that it is also a mark of respect for the dog's owner who felt its loss terribly.

"And the final touch!" says Dr Spicer, wrapping a soft but warm shawl around me, another of her fine things she has loaned to me for the evening. I can hide my tatty old gloves – with holes worn in the fingers – underneath, unseen.

As she smooths the expensive dark wool, I notice that the doctor looks a little tired and drawn. I do hope she is not becoming unwell... But would that be surprising when she has to deal with all the ailments she does, day in, day out? Though Dr Spicer's unsettled manner is *perhaps* due to her concern for Mrs Eriksson at this moment. She has been pleased with the small steps to health that her patient has taken, though none of those steps include going out in daylight and meeting folk just yet! But the doctor is worried that the mine manager's decision to hold a party this evening – to expect Mrs Eriksson to host alongside him – will be altogether too much for the recovering invalid. Still, I do find myself hoping that the young lady will make even a swift appearance. Just so that I might smile at her and let her know that there are people about who might befriend her.

"Ah, and there's my boy," Father proclaims proudly as Lachlan comes out of the bedroom, looking smart in a jacket and trousers and polished boots, his unruly red hair dampened and combed flat to his head.

Dr Spicer breaks into a warm smile at the sight of him. I think that she has become very fond of the two of us over the course of this winter, having no children of her own.

"Well, we'd better be on our way!" says Father, ushering us all out. "Now I know you're not one to be helped, Bridie, but the ground is very slippery with the thaw, so will you take my arm? I don't fancy you falling over and being introduced to the mine bosses half covered in mud!"

"I'll let Lachlan help me," I say, having spotted the frown on my brother's face. I think I would like a chance to see how he is doing. Since the death of Odayan, and his master leaving town, Lachlan has been very low.

Moments later, I am last out and pull the side door closed firmly behind us, and – same as all Hawk's Point residents – I do not bother to lock it as no one living in this small community would dare steal from another. Lachlan holds his arm out to me, and we head into the twilight of this chilly April evening, following behind Father and Dr Spicer.

"Nat's Store looks strange like that, doesn't it?" I say, nodding over to the building.

For once, the store-cum-bar is closed, dark and empty. Mr Nathaniel and Charlie are going to the celebration too, it seems. Seamus and the other miners who lodge there have been turfed out and made to sleep on the floor of the single men's dormitory, while *their* room was hastily tidied and given over to the bosses of the mining company, as they won't be travelling back to the town down the coast till morning.

Lachlan says nothing.

"Are you worried about Charlie being at the gathering tonight?" I ask him. "You do not *have* to talk to him you know. Not if you don't want to."

Charlie has not returned to school yet, despite the crutches that were found for him. He spends his time behind the counter of his father's store, eating as much candy from the jars as he can fit in his face, telling anyone who'll listen how painful his splinted ankle is, and that school is stupid and a waste of his time.

"It's true, I'd rather not be in his company," says Lachlan as we head along the road in the direction of the mining camp and the neat house in the woods nearby. "But I'm more upset about Oskar..."

I think of the lad whose fingers were blown off in the mining blast. It must be a worry to his family to have him hurt so terribly – *and* to have lost his wages.

"Don't worry. I'm sure he'll find something he can do well once he's healed," I say, trying to console my brother. "Though a job heaving a pickaxe and wielding a heavy hammer in the tunnels will not be one of them."

Or wielding a gun as a soldier in the Union Army as Oskar had once hoped, I think to myself.

"It's not that," says Lachlan as we follow in the footsteps of Father and Dr Spicer. "Henni told me today that their father beat Oskar awful bad."

"No!" I gasp. "What for?"

"He found out Oskar was gambling. Some of the older miners were boasting how much money they took off him in card games."

I had forgotten that Henni had mentioned this when we were up on the frozen pond two weeks ago. And I had forgotten what she had started to say that day, before everything went wrong.

"But how can that be? Where would Oskar have got the money from to gamble if he's not working?"

"His father accused him of stealing it from somewhere, though *Oskar* was shouting that it was his fair and square…"

"Dr Spicer, Dr Spicer – come quick!" Easter calls out, running towards us from the top of the path that leads down to the Eriksson's house. "There's a terrible quarrel going on between my master and mistress upstairs. She is dressed and ready but refuses to come down. The master is raging at her. Can you help?"

"I *knew* it would be too much for her," I hear Dr Spicer grumble up ahead as she lifts her skirts and hurries after Easter.

"Well, now … this might be quite an unexpectedly lively evening!" says Father, as we three are left in their trail.

Turning down the path to the mine manager's house, I glimpse the warm flow of lamplight and dark figures at the parlour window. The front door has been left a little ajar and piano music drifts out. Someone is playing a rousing version of a waltz very badly, but I suppose it at least drowns out any arguing going on upstairs.

"Here," I say once we are inside, offering to take Father's overcoat.

In front of us are the stairs, but I can hear no raised voices; perhaps Dr Spicer is doing as hoped and calming the situation? To the right, I can see the kitchen table and chairs already heaving with coats and scarves and hats left on them, and add ours to the pile.

That done, I follow Father and Lachlan into the parlour, where a dozen or so guests mingle; the mining company bosses in expensive suits, while it's Sunday best for the mine foreman and a clerk or two and their wives. But if I look beyond these people and the fug of cigar smoke the gents puff out, I can see *such* things of beauty. Vases, mirrors, paintings … ornate lamps upon finely carved shelves, and a dainty table that holds the centrepiece of the room, a many-layered silver candelabra dotted with a myriad of tiny, twinkling candles. And beside us is the patterned settee I spied Mrs Eriksson lying upon on Christmas Day, only now it is Charlie Nathaniel who takes his ease on it, cradling his crutches and yawning with boredom.

"Now then, this surely is the heroine of the hour!" I vaguely hear someone say and realise – with a gentle nudge and smile from Father – that *I* am being addressed.

The gentleman talking, who has a walrus moustache and a stomach to match, is almost drowned out by the pummelling of the upright mahogany piano as the foreman's wife begins to murder another tune.

By his side is Mr Nathaniel, leaning one hand on the back of the settee. His dark brown waistcoat and jacket strain at the seams to contain his bulk.

"Um, hello. I'm Bridie MacKerrie," I say, shaking the offered hand.

147

"I was just having a very interesting conversation with Mr Nathaniel here," says the gentleman, without bothering to introduce himself to me. "Are you two acquainted?"

He points a crystal glass of amber liquor in the direction of the smug storekeeper. I can imagine that Mr Nathaniel has been boasting of the future he sees for himself. *All* the folk in town are imagining what a grand place Hawk's Point will soon become, with a church, hotel, sawmill, better harbour and trees cut down in swathes to make way for the streets and cabins and stores that will be built. But Mr Nathaniel shouts the loudest about his plans for a large saloon. A proper affair it'll be, he says, with a piano player and tables for card games and perhaps some fine ladies to brighten up the place. Father says he's heard that the storekeeper also fancies himself as mayor of the town too...

"Yes. Mr Nathaniel is a near neighbour of ours," I reply with politeness but no warmth in my voice.

"Well, I was asking him his opinion on what happened with the accidental explosion in the mine, because of his past experience with dynamite," says the gentleman. "You know, before he..."

The gentleman closes one eye and pulls such a strange face, to imitate, I suppose, Mr Nathaniel's injury. I don't care for the storekeeper one bit, but neither do I care for this clumsy mimicking. Mr Nathaniel, however, laughs loudly. Perhaps with his mouth and not his eyes, though…

"You specialised in blasting, Mr Nathaniel?" Father asks him.

"Indeed I did, some years back," the storekeeper replies, sticking his chest out like a preening pigeon. "I worked at several sites down the coast. Was the best in the business and—"

"Anyway," the gentleman interrupts as if he can't be bothered with the story, "Mr Nathaniel tells me that he does not have a theory, but that given the finding of the new mine by *this* little lady, there is not much point in crying over spilt milk. And you know what? He's right – ha!"

I watch as the gentleman guffaws, and notice his moustache is wet at the ends, soaked I suppose in whiskey.

"Mr Nathaniel was also telling me what fools the townspeople are – your good selves excluded, I'm sure!" he continues, once he catches his breath. "He says they put the mine disaster down to some utter nonsense … a curse put on by the spirit of some squaw, I believe!"

Now the man can barely draw breath for laughing, the storekeeper likewise, which is a peculiar thing, since I know for a fact that Mr Nathaniel has been as scared of the supposed Chippewa Curse, and the "woman" he imagined might implement it, as anyone in Hawk's Point.

But I'm suddenly distracted by Lachlan whispering something to me.

"What?" I say, turning to look at him over my shoulder.

"I've just remembered something. Something about Oskar," he hisses, talking – unusually for him – in Gaelic. "I think I might know why he had money to spend."

But Lachlan's whispers, the loud, callous laughter of the mining official, the clumsy clank-and-clunk of the piano ... suddenly I am deaf to them, for Mr and Mrs Eriksson have just entered the room!

Mr Eriksson appears to force a smile, a smile as tight as the grip he has on his wife's arm. His wife has her head held low, but I note her artful blonde curls spilling from a pinned-high bun, her long, swan-like neck, a dress made out of some fine gauzy material, all white, though dotted with delicate blue flowers. She looks frail but remarkable – like a tragic princess from a book of fairy tales, not a sickly wife trapped in a glorified log cabin in a mining town.

Around me, I sense the room quieten as more people become aware of who has arrived in the room.

Behind the young lady I see a concerned Dr Spicer, and an equally worried Easter.

"Come, dear!" Mr Eriksson proclaims loudly. "Let me introduce you to everyone. Everyone, this is my dear wife Katherine."

I am vaguely aware of Lachlan hissing in my ear again, but this is not the time for worrying about Oskar and his gambling debts.

"Katherine," Mr Eriksson continues, leading – somewhat insistently – his wife towards the middle of the room where the soft, dappled candlelight from the centrepiece candelabra is most prettifying. Except that with her unhealthily pale skin, his wife reminds me of nothing more than a barely there, ghostly will-o'-the-wisp, or one of the other phantoms and fairy creatures my sister Effie and so many Highlanders once believed in. "May I introduce you to the gentlemen from the mining company…?"

Mrs Katherine Eriksson continues to keep her glance to the floor as all eyes settle on her and idle chit-chat ceases.

"Bridie!" Lachlan hisses at me yet again, but I pay him no mind. His guess at how Oskar got his money can surely wait.

"Katherine, dear! Won't you say hello to our guests?" asks the mine manager through his forced smile and gritted teeth. "There's Mr Schwarz and Mr Belfonte, and of course Hawk's Point's own little heroine, Bridie MacKerrie!"

In the snap of a second, the young woman looks up – at *me*. She is shaking, her blue eyes pooling with tears. She appears half mad.

Her trembling lips move as if she is about to speak, but first I finally hear what my brother has been trying to tell me.

"It's Miss Kitty!" he mutters.

It's Miss Kitty.

The world slows, the moment freezes.

Four years ago, the new Laird came to our little Scottish island, his haughty wife and spoiled and spiteful daughter by his side, and bit by bit, destroyed the lives of all who lived there. I'd always thought, and always hoped, I'd never have the displeasure of seeing Miss Kitty again, and yet some terrible, twisted piece of invisible thread had brought her here!

"Please…" she begins softly, her dark-rimmed eyes locked on mine, before her voice loudens to a hysterical shriek. "*Please* get them away from me!"

Now screaming, she raises a scrawny bare arm to point at us, as if Father and *I* were a pair of phantoms, or the devil himself and his banshee accomplice.

I feel Lachlan slip his hand in mine and squeeze it. But I am too shocked to squeeze his fingers in reply.

"Katherine!" roars Mr Eriksson, his brow furrowed in distress and distaste. "Be quiet!"

"Get them away from me, I tell you!" the woman

repeats, holding her hand to her throat as if she fears one of us will take a running jump at her and bite the life from her. "He – *that man* tried to murder my father! And he and his family are kidnappers! They stole away a poor young woman from our household!"

My mind: it roars with a loud, raging, repeating word. No, no, *NO*! How can this be happening? How can this reminder of our past difficulties in Scotland have come to us now, to ruin our lives all over again?

"Mrs Eriksson, you are mistaken!" I hear Dr Spicer announce as she hurries forward. "These are my friends, the kind hosts I board with. Please let me help you sit down and—"

The next moment is a blur that is packed with more than is possible to fit in such a small fragment of time. The young woman staggers back against the table, knocking the towering candelabra centrepiece, and a shrill, desperate scream is wrenched from her throat as a glorious halo of brightness illuminates her. Miss Kitty's dress, her delicate, fine-spun dress, is on fire, lit by the dainty candles she has tipped over.

And then instinct takes a hold of me as others stand frozen; I leap towards Kitty and drag her by the hand quick and hard, yelling to someone, anyone – to Easter as it turns out – to pull the front door open.

And with whatever energy I can muster, I tip us both outside on to the snowy, slushy ground. I hear Miss

Kitty's shocked gasps as I roll her this way and that, dousing the flames. And then we are both wretched and panting though I cannot help but see that her delicate white dress has changed to a robe of charred muslin, mud and steam.

I may imagine a silence before the world is full of shouts and helping hands, but in that stillness I feel Kitty cling on to me tight and sob as if she will never stop.

Part of me – the girl who barely escaped my old island home with her life, who watched this person once hit Lachlan about the head – is tempted to peel those thin fingers away now that my duty is done and leave this shocked, pained young woman in the mire.

But whether I like it or not, I have Mother and Father's kindness sewn into my soul.

"*Ist*, now, Miss Kitty," I say softly as I hold my arms around her and let her tears soak into my chest…

CHAPTER 12

Easter suddenly appears on her knees by our side, as fleet and silent as the deer I saw in the woods the day Odayan died.

"Stay still, Miss Kitty! Bridie saved you and the doctor's coming," she entreats her mistress, though she lifts her gaze up long enough to give me a questioning look, clearly struggling to make sense of the shouted accusations she couldn't have helped but hear, along with every other bystander in the room.

I stare back at Easter, hoping she remembers what I have already told her – the untrue accusations Father had hurled at him by the Laird of our island, and the unloved, uncared-for woman that myself and my sisters befriended. When I have the chance, I can talk to her again of how we did *not* kidnap Caroline from Tornish, but instead set her free and that she came very, very gladly.

And of course I stare at Easter with a questioning look too. How have we not known that we had this young woman in common? I suppose I spoke of the Laird, but not his daughter. And for her part, Easter only ever called her 'Mrs Eriksson' in front of me. But if she was so friendly with her mistress, would she not have mentioned us? Would Miss Kitty not have recognised our names? And surely Dr Spicer would have mentioned us too?

"Hester, how *dare* you call your mistress such a familiar name!" I suddenly hear Mr Eriksson roar, as if that is the most pressing point in this moment.

"Your wife needs help, sir!" I shout up at him.

Mr Eriksson ignores me, as if I am as lowly a being as one of the mine ponies.

"Katherine! Get up, for God's sake!" he now shouts at his wife as he runs his hands agitatedly through his white-blond hair, looking quite on the edge of anger. "Hurry and lift my wife up from the ground, Hester! She is *covered* in mud – she cannot be seen like this!"

The man is a fool, and a useless one at that. I saw it during the mine explosion and I see it now. And much as I loathe the young woman cradled in my arms, I pity her too, for being married to such a poor excuse for a husband.

And then our small grouping is surrounded, men folk and their wives pouring from the front door, all shouting, uncertain what to do for the best.

"Let the doctor through!" I hear Mr Nathaniel's gruff

voice shout, and look up to see him ushering Dr Spicer towards us.

And there is the doctor beginning to bend down towards us, before snatching herself straight up again and wincing in pain.

"Are you all right, doc?" asks the storekeeper, taking hold of her elbow.

As his eyes drop down, the worry that knitted his brow turns to a scowl.

Dr Spicer – biting her lip – has put a hand on her stomach. A stomach that is clearly rounded and straining against the loose shirt that she wears.

Wait ... can this be true?

The doctor is expecting a *child*?

But the shock of what I clearly see has its benefits – it sharpens my mind. Before I know it, I have calculated that the doctor is many months pregnant. So she must have already been with child when her poor husband died, I think?

"Can we get Mrs Eriksson to her bedroom, please?" I hear Dr Spicer say, taking a breath and reviving herself. "Lachlan, can you run home and quickly fetch my bag?"

"He can do that and then he can go!" Mr Eriksson suddenly announces. "I will not have him or *his* sort of family anywhere near my own!"

And all of a sudden, hands reach down to drag Miss

Kitty from my care, and though she tries to hold tight, though her red-rimmed blue eyes beseech me, she is lifted away and I am left in the soft, snowy mud, feeling peculiarly bereft … till I hear a terrible sound.

A bear-like roar comes out of the woods and we all turn in terror to see what is hurtling towards us.

With a muddle of swearing and shouts of "He told me! He told me you made him do it!" Oskar's father rushes at Mr Nathaniel, fists colliding with his face…

The storekeeper stumbles to the ground, with Oskar's father quickly on top of him, pummelling and raging.

"You bribed my son to do something *so* dangerous, and look at the mess of him now! Look at the others who were hurt!"

"Grab him! Pull him back!" the mine manager orders his foreman and clerks, like a general barking at foot soldiers and not getting his own hands dirty.

I see the men hesitate and glance at each other quickly. I think they are none the wiser about what has provoked this attack, but are a little pleased to see the despised Mr Nathaniel get his comeuppance. Still, Mr Eriksson pays their wages and after a moment they spring into action and do as they are told, tearing Oskar and Henni's father away from the bleeding-nosed storekeeper.

"Good God, man!" says one of the mining company gentlemen. "How *dare* you set upon

Mr Nathaniel like this!"

"You ask how I dare?" the miner answers panting, his arms pinned back. "How does this man dare to *pay* my son to set an explosion? An explosion that could have killed *all* of us in the tunnels?"

"Don't be ridiculous!" Mr Eriksson bellows, his eyes quite wild.

The next person who speaks startles everyone.

"It's not ridiculous!" says Lachlan, stepping forward. "The morning of the explosion, Mr Nathaniel made me run an errand and take a package to Oskar. I wasn't supposed to look inside, but I did. It was money."

And now my shocked and skittish mind darts to confirm the truth of what has gone on... Mr Nathaniel boasted of his former skill working with explosives. And didn't Easter and I overhear him tell Mr Eriksson on Christmas Day to sort things at the mine, to make it more profitable, or *he* would? How he'd pay someone off to make it happen? And that foolish person turned out to be Henni's gullible brother...

"Rubbish!" Mr Eriksson shouts in my brother's face.

"No, it *is* true." I jump to my brother's defence. "Ask Oskar. Ask the Irish miner Seamus – *he* knows. Mr Nathaniel asked him first, but he turned him down."

"Nonsense. Seamus knows nothing. He's an addle-headed drunk," mutters the storekeeper as he's helped to his feet.

"What the hell is going on here?" the other gentleman from the mining company demands.

"Lies! *That* is what is going on here!" Mr Eriksson shouts out. "Someone tie up that thug, and Mr MacKerrie, take your urchins away from here. These accusations against Mr Nathaniel are ridiculous. Why would he do such a thing?"

"Come away," says Father, urging my brother and me toward the path. "No one is in a position to listen to reason right now. I'll come back and talk to Mr Eriksson in the morning and sort things out…"

But the three of us pause as we hear what is said next.

"Mr Schwarz, Mr Belfonte, I'm guilty!" Mr Nathaniel suddenly announces.

Pebbles on the path crunch as Father, Lachlan and I turn around at this strange turn of events.

"Yes, indeed, I am guilty of paying the lad to lay the extra explosion," says Mr Nathaniel, looking surprisingly sorrowful. "It was a desperate act to find more copper fast, since the mine was failing."

Everyone is standing in a silent tableau in that moment, framed by the soft light from inside the house and the haze of smoke from the fire that must have now been put out in the parlour.

"But hear *this*, gentlemen, I am just a humble storekeeper," Mr Nathaniel continues, wiping the blood from his nose with the back of his hand. "I would *never* have thought to do something so shocking and dangerous on my own. Mr Eriksson *ordered* me to make it happen. *He* is behind the terrible disaster that happened. The burden of guilt is all his!"

Well, I knew Mr Nathaniel was capable of many things, but being such an actor is quite the surprise. And I can see from the reactions of all around him – folk staring in hatred at the startled mine manager – that his role of humble sidekick has been a great success...

Father, Lachlan and I leap to our feet as soon as we hear the creaking drag of the latch lift in the parlour's side door.

"How is she?" asks Father in concern, rushing to take the heavy leather bag from a clearly exhausted Dr Spicer.

I glance at him, thinking what a good man he is. Back on the island, Miss Kitty's father would have happily seen *mine* flung in prison or hanged, supposing him to have masterminded an attack planned by the desperate young men of the island. And now the very same Laird's daughter has unlocked our box of secrets in front of everyone, letting them slither and slip from their hiding places for all to gawp at and gossip over, as they no doubt will. And yet Father enquires as to her health.

If only *I* could be as good as him. But while we've sat

here awaiting Dr Spicer's return, I have remembered Easter telling me that her mistress's father was dead. And knowing that the Laird – the truly heartless Mr Palmer-Reeves – is no longer of this earth has given me *considerable* pleasure, I'm not ashamed to say. His death obviously resulted in Miss Kitty and her mother moving to London. But what did it mean for the islanders that remained on Tornish? Are their lives better with the Laird gone? Are any of them, my friend Will's family included, still there...?

"When the flames shot upwards, they burnt off some of Mrs Eriksson's hair at the back, but in general she is not too badly hurt, thanks to Bridie's quick actions," says Dr Spicer, letting me take her coat and fur hat from her. "She is more in shock, from the accident *and* from the arguing and upsets of the evening."

"Including seeing us?" I ask, hanging her things on the pegs by the door.

"Including seeing you," says Dr Spicer, easing herself gratefully on to the chair by the stove and taking the mug of coffee Lachlan has just poured for her. "I didn't realise, but she recognised your names when Easter and I had mentioned you all. She hoped never to meet you."

"By staying inside her house *forever*?" asks Lachlan, settling himself at her feet.

"By staying inside till the first steamship of the

spring, when she planned to leave both Hawk's Point and her husband," says the doctor, to all our surprise. "Mrs Eriksson admitted that to me just now. She also admitted that she was so terrified of seeing you all at the party that she was quite out of her wits, and panicked. I very quickly set her right about the accusations she made."

I see a look pass between Dr Spicer and Father – and that look tells me that he has trusted the doctor with our secrets during their long evening talks this winter.

"Well, thank you for telling her the truth of our situation," says Father. "I will try doing the same with her husband tomorrow. But how are *you*, Stephanie?"

Now, from that use of her first name and the gentle question he asks, I can tell that Dr Spicer has already shared her *own* secret with Father.

"I'm well, thank you," she says, putting her hand to the dome of her stomach. "Just tired and sometimes uncomfortable, as mothers-to-be often are at this stage."

"Why, if I may ask, didn't you tell us?" I say, talking of myself and Lachlan. "I mean, it is clearly wonderful news that you and your husband are to be parents. I mean, *you*. I mean— I mean, I'm so very sorry that your husband will not know his own son or daughter..."

Dr Spicer smiles at me, forgiving my clumsy stutters and stumbles.

"Well, this might amuse you, Bridie, since I'm

medically trained and *should* know better, but I did not realise till a week or so ago that I *was* with child!" she admits, appearing a little shamefaced. "I was so very lost in the time after Frank died, and then so very busy in the last few months here, that I did not think clearly. I had no idea of this miracle I'd been blessed with."

"You never thought you'd be a mother, did you?" Lachlan asks, gazing up at her.

For a moment Dr Spicer says nothing, just smiles at my brother, almost as a mother might.

"No, I did not," she says finally, patting Lachlan's arm before she continues. "I did tell your father, however, as I wanted to talk to him about how the townspeople might take the news. They struggled to accept me as a female doctor, and it did make me worry what they'd make of a female doctor who was expecting a child!"

"Well, as I said, it might take folk by surprise," Father says, scratching his beard. "But I'm sure in time they'll be glad for you."

"After tonight I have my doubts," Dr Spicer answers him. "Once I finished treating his wife I was informed by Mr Eriksson that I would not be welcome back in his house. So perhaps I might have to think about returning to Philadelphia…"

"What?" says Father, his eyebrows bending into a deep frown.

"But why did he say you would not be welcome?"

I ask. "Because you're to have a baby? Or because of what Miss Kitty – Mrs Eriksson – said about *us*?"

"A little of both, I think," she admits. "All I can be sure of is that Mr Eriksson decided on the spot that a lone woman expecting a child – who lives under the same roof as a would-be murderer and a family of kidnappers – was not someone who should be trusted with his wife's care."

She gives us all a wry smile, as if she – a woman of science and reason – can barely believe the stupidity of what's happened.

"I think Mr Eriksson is both furious and frightened that Mr Nathaniel has placed the blame of the mine-tunnel explosion at his feet," Father suggests. "And so he has taken out his anger on *you* it seems, and us too."

"But surely Mr Nathaniel won't get away with pushing the blame away from himself," I say angrily at the injustice. "Surely he—"

My words are interrupted by a soft but insistent tapping at the side door.

There is a whimpering too.

We all look at each other but being so close to the door already, I quickly wrestle it open. And there … there in the light that pools from our tiny parlour stands Miss Kitty, wrapped in her black fur cape and with the curls of her once neat hair now wilted and singed about her shoulders. She is held up by a person on either side.

One is Easter, the other is – and I can barely breathe for the surprise of it – Jean.

As for the whimpering? A little of it comes from Miss Kitty to be sure, but the louder whimpers come from the two husky pups peeking out of Jean's knapsack...

CHAPTER 13

I look from Miss Kitty to Jean and back again. I would *never* have expected either of them to be sitting as guests in our parlour tonight, for very different reasons.

Yet here they are.

Jean's reason for returning to Hawk's Point was that he was paid to drive the sled and the dogs that brought the mine company's men here. He will be gone in the morning, not to return. As for the two pups he brought with him from his visit to the reservation, he is keeping one, already named Odayan, and gifting the other to Lachlan.

"What will I call you?" my brother cries and laughs as he holds the deliciously furry, fat, wriggling creature in his hands, ignoring the rest of us in the room.

"What did you call your last dog?" I hear Jean ask.

"Patch!" Lachlan laughs, rubbing noses with the pup. "I'll call you Patch!"

We leave the gaiety to my brother and the puppies who now all roll and play together on the floor. It is time to turn our attention to Miss Kitty, who has once again been checked over by Dr Spicer in the room we share, and now − sitting in the chair by the stove − seems somewhat revived by a tin mug of sweetened coffee that Father has given her.

"You are not in too much pain, my dear?" Dr Spicer asks.

"Only in my heart," she says, shivering. "I cannot *bear* to be near that man for a moment longer."

"After Dr Spicer left, Mr Eriksson was very agitated," says Easter, who is seated next to Miss Kitty. "He didn't seem to care much about how his own wife was. He seemed more troubled about going back downstairs to face the men from the mine company and Mr Nathaniel."

"Mr Nathaniel was still there?" I ask, thinking the storekeeper would have disappeared pretty quickly after his accusation.

"He was sitting downstairs on the settee, bold as brass, drinking all the brandy and telling the mining company gentlemen about his poor injured son," Easter says with sarcasm dripping from her words. "But before Mr Eriksson rejoined them all, Miss Kitty said something to him."

She nudges her mistress.

"I told my husband that I knew he was involved," Miss Kitty says, gripping her tin mug tight in one hand.

LITTLE BIRD LANDS

"I said I saw him at his desk counting out money one day when he thought me fast asleep on the settee. Next day, I watched from my bedroom window as he passed the money to Mr Nathaniel, standing waiting outside. When he heard that, my husband looked at me most murderously…"

"He did," Easter confirms. "As soon as he stormed out of the room, we both looked at each other and knew we had to leave. We took a few things and crept out the back door…"

I see Father frown and realise I am frowning deeply too. The truth is, I may have hated Miss Kitty with a vengeance when I was younger, but this person in front of me today is a pathetic, bedraggled version of the girl she once was, and does not frighten me one bit. Also, I am aware that Easter and Dr Spicer both have some fondness, as well as pity, for the troubled invalid they have both cared for in their different ways.

But wait: what are Easter and Miss Kitty saying exactly? Where are they to go? Do they mean to ask to stay *here*? As this startling thought comes to me, Miss Kitty appears to droop, like a cut flower out of water. By comparison, Easter sits up straight by her side, like a strong reed in a buffeting stream.

"Miss Kitty has something to tell you," she says, patting the young woman's arm as if urging her on.

"You – you have to understand, Mr MacKerrie,"

says Miss Kitty directing her words to Father, "that it was a shock when I heard about Scots folk come to town, and then realised it was *your* family. I felt very confused and troubled because, you see, I have always tried to persuade myself that my papa was a good and noble man. But tonight, as Dr Spicer attended to me and explained your side of things, I realised he was … not."

"Go on: tell them what your father was like," I hear Easter mutter to her.

"Papa, for all that he might spoil and indulge Mama and me … you see, he was just as quick to be in terrible tempers with us. Mama to this *day* has a small scar *here* from when Papa threw a china cup at her."

Miss Kitty raises her free hand and gestures to a spot above her right eyebrow.

"And he cared for *nothing* but money. How to get it, how to gamble it away," she continues, glancing occasionally at Easter for reassurance. "When his heart gave out and Mama went to sell Tornish, we found that a large amount of what he left us had to be used to pay his debts. We took what little remained and went to London … where I met my husband."

Emotions are fickle things. Like a brisk easterly wind that races along only to change direction in an instant, emotions can switch around and have you see things quite differently. For these last few years, the news of the Laird's wife and daughter's fall from grace would have sounded like sweet revenge indeed. And yet now pity pinches at my heart to hear that she grew up with one bully and married another.

And something *else* pinches at my heart too, a burning, questioning curiousity.

"After your Father died and Tornish was sold, who bought the island?" I interrupt Miss Kitty. "And the families there ... were they all well when you were last there?"

Her red-rimmed eyes turn to me. "Oh, but there was *no one* left on the island. Father had them all removed when he turned the place into a hunting ground. And the Englishman who bought the island was some rich man that had once come to shoot the deer Father bred."

In that crushing moment I try not to be overwhelmed with sadness thinking of that once bustling island now empty of *all* the folk we knew. All except dear Mother, who lies quietly at her rest in the churchyard there.

"I'm sorry that I shouted out against you when I saw you all," mutters Miss Kitty, sinking into herself in her awkwardness. "When my husband made me come into the parlour, I couldn't bear to think what you would remember of me..."

I see Lachlan glance up at that, remembering the blow she once gave him about the head. Jean – even though he knows nothing of our history – puts a calming hand on my brother's shoulder, and I am grateful to him for it.

"Course I lost my parents too young to know for sure," Easter speaks up, "but don't children generally learn their manners – or lack of 'em – from their parents? And from what Miss Kitty says, her own father was *not* the best of men."

"Well said, Easter," Dr Spicer praises my friend. "It is no excuse, but it is always wise to consider the *reason* for people's behaviour."

Then Mr Nathaniel and his son must come from a very long line of mean-spirited, low-minded ancestors, I think to myself darkly.

"And … and so I am set on leaving my husband," I hear Miss Kitty say. "I will tell him to give me my steamship fare and enough money that I might set myself up with a little apartment in Chicago."

"You are sure he will do that?" Jean asks dubiously, glancing up from the stool he sits on, puppies and Lachlan playing at his feet. The paws and snout of one puppy are black from chewing on a half-burnt piece of kindling that has fallen out of the pot-bellied stove.

"He *will* if he wants his wife to keep her mouth shut and not have the shame of her confirming his involvement in the mine collapse – and of his neglect of her!" Easter says very surely.

"But my dear," Dr Spicer says to Miss Kitty, "even if

he gives you enough money for accommodation, how will you live?"

"Well, I have some jewellery I can sell," she answers, shakily taking a small bulging bag from the pocket of her skirt. "And I shall have to find myself a little job, I suppose..."

Despite the strange and serious turn this evening has taken, I nearly laugh out loud. What on *earth* can a pampered, petted creature such as Miss Kitty *do* exactly? Who would rush to give her *any* kind of employment?

And then my merriment sinks away when I realise that if *Miss Kitty* is to leave, then Easter must be set on going too...

"You are bound for Chicago?" I say, a crushing weight squeezing my chest as I begin to miss my friend already.

"No, not at all!" Easter says with a cheerful laugh, pulling a well-worn letter from her apron pocket. "Miss Kitty will make sure Mr Eriksson settles on my wages due, then I'm headed west!"

My heart skips as if excitement is a living thing in my chest.

"West, you say?" I hear Father ask her.

"Yes! I know some fine folk that have settled there. Mrs Clarice Campbell and her husband – they are in a town in Minnesota called..." Easter stops to read the details of the letter she unfolds.

"…Hopetown … Hope*toun*."

"Hopetoun, eh? You know, Hopetoun is the name of a wee place in Scotland, near Edinburgh," says Father, his face brightening, his rusty-red eyebrows raised high. "How are these folks, the Campbells, finding it there? Are they homesteading?"

My heart begins to lift; Father might just have glimpsed an invisible thread. A fine one, for sure, barely there, really… He mistakenly thinks that these Campbells Easter speaks of must be directly from Scotland with such a name, rather than a black American couple that have inherited it as a matter of chance and circumstance down the years, in the same way Jean has his French name. But at this moment I am not about to explain that to him. For is Minnesota not a place of prairies and far horizons? Dare I hope that Father is thinking that particular state may be a better, happier place for us to settle after what has happened here tonight?

"Here, come let us see if we can find this town," says Father, ushering Easter away through to the storefront schoolroom where a large map of America is nailed to the wall. I'm about to follow when Miss Kitty asks something of me.

"Excuse me," she says, rather shyly. "What became of Miss Caroline? Do you know?"

"Why yes," I reply. "She married Samuel Mitford, the artist who came to paint your father's portrait. They were in Glasgow for a while but are now in London I believe, with my sister Ishbel."

"Really? My mother and I spent a summer in Glasgow, two or three years ago, before Father died," Miss Kitty recounts.

I don't tell her that I saw them both from a distance once, attending an entertainment in the park arranged by Effie's mistress Mrs Lennox. But still, now that I recall that time, I realise Miss Kitty might unwittingly hold a clue to what happened to my other sister…

"Amongst the society ladies you met in Glasgow, do you remember a Mrs Lennox?" I ask.

"Mrs Lennox?" murmurs Miss Kitty.

"She did a lot of charity work," I try to prompt her.

"Yes, yes I do!" she says, suddenly becoming more animated. "Mother and I didn't know her well, but we took tea with her on occasion at other ladies' houses."

My heart lurches. To speak of Mrs Lennox seems to make a long-lost invisible thread of my own come trembling into view, bringing me closer to Effie than I have been in a very long time.

"Ah, I remember now … it was terribly sad," Miss Kitty chatters on. "Just before we went back to Tornish, we heard that Mrs Lennox had come down with influenza and died after only a few days. One minute she was doing wonderful work for the poor, the next her house is shut up and sold off, just like that."

And just like that, the invisible thread I have been imagining is broken, snapped, and my heart with it. So Effie never got my letters. They must have lain on the dusty doormat of the empty house till the new owners tossed them aside, not remotely interested in who the Miss Effie MacKerrie on the envelope might have been. But where on earth did she go? To London, to be with Ishbel, Caroline and Samuel? But then, what happened to the letter I sent to *them*?

"Bridie! Bridie! What do you think, my love?" I suddenly become aware of Father saying.

I look up to see him grinning ear to ear in the doorway through to the storefront.

"I know it sounds like a crazy scheme, but should we do this? Didn't you always dream of it?"

I try to smile at him while my mind quickly grapples with his meaning, hoping it is what I think it is.

"Shall we go west, my Bridie?"

This small heart of mine, it may never quite mend at the loss of my sisters, especially when it breaks a little every time I think too hard of them. But what Father has just said, it goes a long way to healing me.

I gulp away the pained knot of sadness in my throat and give him a grateful smile.

"Yes, Father," I tell him. "Let us go west…"

I glance around at our peculiar collection of people (and pups!) in the parlour, and know that in a week or so, as the first steamship of spring comes puffing to Hawk's Point harbour and leaves again, we will all be gone, beginning our separate new stories.

Perhaps Mr Eriksson's days in the town are numbered too if he has so dreadfully disgraced himself in the eyes of the mining company. Meanwhile the oily Mr Nathaniel will be rubbing his hands together, eyeing up the position of mine manager himself, perhaps, along with his other grand plans!

Sadly, I guess there is no point expecting Mr Schwarz or Mr Belfonte to believe a lowly miner like Oskar's father, or believe anything my *own* father or Lachlan or I were to say about the storekeeper and his guilt – not with our characters so tarnished. But how desperately unfair is it that a man with such a tainted soul as Mr Nathaniel can get away scot-free?

Isn't it unspeakably unfair that good people might *never* expect the goodness they are due, or that a sour-hearted, mean-spirited man such as Mr Nathaniel might *never* face the justice and punishment he deserves?

But that is sadly the way of our world, is it not?

And yet ... and yet *perhaps* there is one small act of vengeance I can take pleasure in.

For Nat's Store will this moment still be empty, I think. And like everyone's home in town, the back door will likely remain unlocked.

"I'll fetch a few more logs to burn," I mutter, getting

up and pretending to examine how the fire in the stove is going.

Father, Dr Spicer, Miss Kitty and Easter are talking again, and my brother is too busy with the pups to pay me any attention as I snatch Lachlan's collection of crows' feathers from the small jar on the shelf.

Only Jean watches me wordlessly as I now quickly bend to pick up the charred stick that one of the pups has lost interest in.

"I will help you with the wood," says Jean, standing up and following me to the door as I open it.

"There's no need," I tell him, then quietly ask him a question. "But can you tell me how to call someone 'evil' in Chippewa?"

Jean lets his gaze fall to the items I hold then looks me straight in the eye.

"You might call a man an evil spirit, or devil," he says, summing up the storekeeper very well. "We'd say '*maji-manidoo*'..."

"Thank you," I tell him as I turn right out of the side door when the wood pile lies to the left.

I'll have to be quick, and I'll have to remember to bring in some logs on my return so no one guesses the mischief I have been up to.

And when I am seated in the parlour again in a few minutes' time, I'll listen out for the eventual slam of the front door of Nat's Store, whenever Mr Nathaniel and Charlie and their guests from the mining company amble back.

And I will strain to hear the shouts of alarm that will surely ring out when the storekeeper finds that the ghost of the Indian maiden has paid him a call, leaving a blackened word scrawled on his pillow with a charred stick and a trail of black feathers scattered about his bed as a warning that *someone* knows the truth of his wicked lies.

For all of the injured miners' sakes, for Easter's sake, for *all* our sakes', I wish the superstitious Mr Nathaniel much dread, fear and nightmares, and I am happy to deliver them to him...

MINNESOTA,
1865

CHAPTER 14

I stretch my wings wide and glide, feathers skimming
the blue morning haze that hovers over a shape-shifting,
evergreen sea of treetops.

The snow is fading fast from the mountains and
valleys, from the forest upon forest that goes on as far as
the eye can see.

It is truly beautiful.

I'm sorry it does not feel like home.

And so I turn in my flight path to face the silver span
of the lake and gently flap my wings, speeding up with
every beat, chasing the ship that ploughs through the
water, with drifting puffs of steam as its flag.

Like a great iron arrow, the ship will point me where
I need to go.

To the place where I can finally land…

And then my dreamings of leaving Michigan and
Hawk's Point scatter in an instant as gunshots and
screams wake me.

"What's happening?" I ask in alarm, struggling to sit

up from the rough mattress and get my balance in the rocking, rattling wagon.

Directly in front of me, in the open hooped arch of the white canvas roof, I see Dr Spicer – or her back at least – as she struggles to hold the reins steady.

On my hands and knees, I scramble over to her, the puppy Patch jumping beside me as if this is an excellent game.

But where are the others?

And what is this? Are we under attack by ruffian bushwackers, out to steal from us? Or have we stumbled upon a skirmish between Union and Confederate soldiers? Though how can *that* be when we are so very, very far from where the fighting is taking place?

With a last heave I lean across the wooden bench that Dr Spicer sits upon and grapple for the reins, but Father, who has been walking alongside and leading the horses, has already got hold of Sultan's halter, while the less skittish Queenie whinnies her disapproval of the terrible noise. I cannot see Pip, the piebald pony that Dr Spicer bought from a farmer on the way here, *or* Lachlan, who was riding Pip the last I saw before I fell asleep. What I *can* make out are the wooden buildings of a town up ahead, and the figures of a milling, roaring crowd. So at least no attack is aimed directly at *us* … but what business is happening up ahead? And where exactly are we?

"Is this it? Are we at Hopetoun at last?" I ask, though the doctor has not yet answered my first questions.

Before she can say a word, there is another rat-a-tat-tat of gunfire, though it now sounds to me peculiar, each bang coming far too fast after the other, faster than any shotgun can be reloaded.

Another frightened scream rings out.

Is *this* how it is to be? We have journeyed all this way, these last three weeks, only to find our destination is *not* a happy ending but a battleground of some kind?

But then I see Easter to the right of the wagon, arms swinging by her sides as she walks, looking back over her shoulder and shouting to someone unseen, "It's only firecrackers! Ain't you heard any before?"

"Whoa!" Father is calling out and brings the two horses to a standstill. "Firecrackers, you think, Easter? Must be some kind of celebration then. Maybe they knew we were coming and wanted to welcome us!"

With Easter's knowledge and Father's joking, my frantically thumping heart begins to slow and to steady.

Ah, and *now* here is Lachlan, coming trotting alongside us on Pip.

"Are you all right?" he asks of Dr Spicer.

"Of course!" she replies, as if my brother's concern is a little ridiculous.

I swear the doctor is becoming more stubbornly independent the bigger her belly gets. And I don't just mean in her last-minute decision to head west to Minnesota with us instead of heading back east. I mean she has been *especially* driven to prove that a woman in her condition is as capable as the rest of us; as able to take a turn walking and not riding in the wagon, as able to squat down to wash clothes in a river or cook over an open fire.

"Hold on, I feel stiff – I'm going to walk," I call out so that Father doesn't urge the horses on before I have a chance to grab the pup and clamber down on to the wild-grass verged trail that leads to the settlement ahead.

Happy to be free, floppy-eared Patch lollops on, leading the way as the wagon rumbles forward. I lollop a little myself, trying to hide that I am limping. The miles and miles of walking have taken their toll on my twisted foot, but I suppose I am as stubborn as Dr Spicer and have admitted the fact to no one.

Ignoring the jarring ache in my ankle, I take a quick look at the wooden buildings we approach: several houses and cabins at first, next a lumber yard, a blacksmith and then many stores that I cannot yet make out due to the crowds and the horses and carts that are halted in the street.

The folk ahead are too caught up in whatever excites them to notice our arrival. Except for one tall woman, her black hair scraped into a neat, low bun at the nape of her neck, her skin dark against a striped, pale-blue dress and white apron. She holds a hand to her brow, staring our way.

And what does she see? What must our little party look like? A great rollicking wagon like ours being driven by a heavily pregnant woman – it must be an unusual sight, I would think. And the fierce red hair of Father and Lachlan cannot easily be missed. With my own black hair long and loose as usual, perhaps from a distance I might look a little like an *Anishinaabe* girl and not the scrawny Scottish lass I am in truth. For I have glimpsed my reflection in mother's old hand mirror in the wagon and watched as the skin of my cheeks and nose burnt first pink, then turned nut-brown, from the glare of the spring sunshine and my wilful lack of bonnet.

Then there's Easter waving a wary Miss Kitty to come on now, since there's nothing to be feared of, and the two of them falling companionably together like sisters, though one is as dark-skinned as the other is milk pale. And all of us – no matter how we tried to keep ourselves clean as we travelled – are coated in a light layer of dust from the churning of the wagon wheels as we jiggled and journeyed our way here.

"Mrs Campbell? MRS CAMPBELL!" Easter calls out suddenly.

The watching woman stares harder, then puts a hand

to her mouth in surprise as my friend begins to run towards her.

"Easter? EASTER!" The lady gathers herself together enough to call back before turning to a heavyset man who stands laughing at the high jinks and tomfoolery going on in the street. "Solomon, look who has come to us!"

I slow, smiling at the scene of reunion, while Father ties Sultan to a wooden rail next to a small but smart-looking, sided wagon with gilt letters upon it: "Jakob Wahle, Photographer". The vehicle next to it is larger, with seats inside and a hand-painted sign that reads "Minnesota Stage Company". We have been locked away in the snowy world of Hawk's Point for so long – not to mention the endless trails here through woods and wild-flower prairies – that the busyness and noise of this place seems quite bedazzling.

"Well, so let's see if we can find out what's afoot here!" says Father, carefully helping Dr Spicer down from the wagon.

The tone of his voice is bright but I see he looks nervous. On the way west, Father had talked of what a fine thing it was that Mrs Clarice Campbell had written such a detailed letter to her young friend Easter, telling her how good the land around Hopetoun was and how many homesteads were still available to purchase. But I wonder if he worries that in the year since the letter was sent, many more people like us will have come and there may be *no* land left to claim?

And at this moment, my own cheerfulness deserts me as I realise I very much need to answer a call of nature. Out in the wild it is so easy to discreetly hide behind a tree or dip into the waist-high prairie grasses. Oh, how I *wish* I hadn't dropped off to sleep when I took a turn resting in the wagon! Where am I to go here in town when I know no one?

Though I remind myself that *Easter* does. I must be brave and ask Mrs Campbell for assistance, I think.

And so once Lachlan has tied up Pip and scooped up his little dog, he and I follow Father and Dr Spicer. Together we make our way towards the couple who seem so very delighted to set eyes upon the foundling they first came across at the pastor's house and church in Chicago. As we reach them, Easter is just breaking away from a tight, tearful hug.

"I would've written to you, Mrs Campbell, only we've been cut off *all* winter in Michigan," she tells the older woman. "We just came out on the first ship of the spring and figured we might get here quicker than any letter!"

Mr and Mrs Campbell, they "ahh!" and they "ohh!" as she speaks but look on curiously at her strange troupe of travelling companions. Becoming suddenly aware of the need for introductions, Easter turns first to the young lady who stands next to her.

"This is Miss Kitty," says Easter. "She *was* my mistress in the mining town but not any more."

On the day of departure from Hawk's Point, I think we all knew that the clearly terrified Miss Kitty would never manage a minute alone in Chicago. She was pathetically grateful when Father and Dr Spicer suggested she join us on our adventuring.

"Pleased to meet you," Miss Kitty trills in her best cut-glass English voice, oh-so-delicately holding out her hand to shake Mr and Mrs Campbell's. She does try very hard to hold on to her niceties and manners, even when she is as filthy and as much in need of a bath as *any* of us after our long journey.

"And this is Dr Spicer," Easter continues.

Mr Campbell reaches a hand out to Father, who quickly corrects the mistake by turning to the *real* doctor.

"Dr Stephanie Spicer, pleased to meet you," says our friend, stepping forward to shake Mr Campbell's offered hand.

"And *these* folks are from Scotland," Easter adds, turning to us with a wide smile. "This is Mr Robert MacKerrie, Lachlan and Bridie…"

Mr and Mrs Campbell look what you might call *bamboozled*. I dare say they are confused as to who is kin to who and what relationship we might be to one another. Together we must appear like the mismatched creatures of the "Happy Family" exhibit back at Barnum's American Museum in New York City!

But the Campbells are not the only ones to be bamboozled. For we have yet to find out the cause of the revelry going on about the town. I suspect Father is about to ask when I realise I can wait patiently and politely not a moment longer, and step myself closer to Mrs Campbell's side.

"Excuse me, might you know of a privy I could use?" I ask in a low voice.

"Uh, yes, of course," Mrs Campbell replies. "This is our store here – you'll find the privy out back."

As I turn, I take a fleeting look at the wooden storefront, and through the open door I see long thick bolts of patterned cloth stacked one on top of another, as well as men's suits hanging up and dressmaking paraphernalia piled on a counter.

"I'll come with you!" Easter calls out, quickly catching me up as I head down the scruffy, weed-strewn alley between the Campbell's building and the one next to it.

The door to the privy is a little open and I am quickly inside, much to my relief.

"Did you see all the things in the store?" I hear Easter say as she waits her turn on the other side of the rough-planked door. "It looks like such a grand sort of place, doesn't it? I remember Mrs Campbell saying she was a seamstress back east. She and Mr Campbell must have decided to continue in that trade."

"But why would they do that?" I ask as I fix myself up and step out of the privy. "I thought they'd come out here to homestead."

"Maybe they realised they were better shopkeepers than farmers," I hear Easter reply as we swap places and she disappears inside.

Now that I am able to relax, I find myself staring out at the countryside that lies beyond the town. I step across the scrubby back lot to take a better look at the soft green-and-gold prairie dotted with the gentle rise of a tree-covered hill here and there. Marvelling at the cloudless blue sky that seems more enormous than is possible, I take a few steps further and see a cheerful tumble of yellow-headed flowers at my feet. I pick a small bunch and smell their light scent of newly woken spring.

"What a long way we have come, eh, Mother?" I mutter softly, thinking of the wildflowers I'd sometimes pick and place on her grave.

A sharp cough suddenly sends me spinning around to see a gentleman standing at the back of the neighbouring building, his hands placed on a great, wooden camera fixed to three wooden legs.

"My apologies, I did not want to startle you," he

says, touching his hand to the brim of his neat felt hat. "But I felt I should let you know I was here."

"Oh, I … no, I mean yes, thank you," I answer flustered, wondering what he must have made of me chattering to no one of this world. "Is that your wagon out front? You take tintype photographs?"

Jakob something, the sign on the side had proclaimed. His voice has a clipped sound to it, akin to the voices of Henni and Matilde I think. So he might be German perhaps, or Bohemian, or Austrian?

"Yes, I do travel the country taking tintypes," he says. "But this … this is my *new* camera, which takes very special photographs. And what a perfect day to use it!"

"What kind of photographs does it take?" I ask.

The young man's face lights up. "Well, you see, I take several pictures of the same scene, focussing a little differently each time. And then I will develop the negatives and do what is called a 'combination print'. The finished image is very different from a tintype; it is as if it has the qualities of a painting."

I smile, understanding nothing of what he says. But I like the brightness in his eyes as he speaks.

"May I take your image? Miss…"

Just call me Bridie, I'm about to say – when something stirs in me and a different name altogether comes to my lips.

"I am called Little Bird," I tell him, pushing the hair

back from my face, defying him to ask for a more usual, expected name.

"Well, Miss ... Little Bird," he says with a lift of his eyebrows, "the light of the landscape behind you and the darkness of your hair, it would make a pleasing composition I think."

I nod yes – I can see no reason why not. And perhaps I am vain enough to be pleased to be chosen to pose for him.

"Stay as you are!" he tells me, picking up his camera and its stand and bringing them closer to me. "But look off to the side, please. And keep very still for the exposure, and so I can change plates..."

I lift my weaker hand to my chest, clutching my posy, almost daring the photographer to comment on it or ask me to change hands, but he says nothing. So I begin to relax and turn my head as he has asked, wondering if the vista I look at is facing west. The wind whips up a little, lifting my hair with it, and I remember that chilly day on the top of the Glas Crags when I stared off in the direction of America, thinking I would never in all my life travel there. Ha!

"Finished! Thank you," says the photographer after no time at all.

As I ease my pose, I see that my friend is standing with her hands on her hips, smiling at me.

"I heard you say that it was a 'perfect' day to use your

new camera," Easter says to the young man. "What is the celebration about on the street?"

The photographer looks from Easter to me and back again, seeming almost shocked.

"You do not know?" he asks.

"We've been travelling and are newly arrived," I tell him.

The photographer's face breaks into a smile as he announces, "The war is over! The news just came to town this morning!"

"The North won?" I check, though how can it be otherwise with the jubilation we witnessed on the street?

"Yes, the North – the Union Army – won," he assures us with a very certain nod as he folds up the legs of his camera stand and lifts the whole contraption to his shoulder.

Oh, my … what a thing, what a thing! Soldiers – like Marthy-Jane's dear papa – can lay down their arms and make their way back home after four long, hard years of fighting. And for the slaves of the south, in their prison of tobacco and cotton plantations, this day is beyond imagining. Their lives and their children's lives will be forever changed!

"Bridie! Easter! Come quick!" I hear Miss Kitty call out sharply down the side of the building.

Together we two girls hoick up our skirts and run

back toward the main street.

"You'll never guess the news!" Miss Kitty says excitedly, with a smile as bright as noon-day sunshine.

"The war is done with – we've just been told!" I reply, indicating towards the photographer who has followed us down the alley and begun to set up his camera again. "But what is happening here?"

The crowd have gathered around something or someone. As they begin to hush, I hear the clear notes ring out from Father's tin whistle and Lachlan begin to sing a Gaelic air in his sweet, high voice. Quickly I hurry around the blurred edge of the townspeople the better to see my father and brother.

"Is this your Scots language?" asks Easter, following close at my heels. "What do they sing of?"

My mind is a jumble and muddle of joy at what we have so recently heard, but translating from Gaelic to English is as simple as breathing.

"It is a Scottish poem, turned to music. In Gaelic it's called '*Is Braithrean Sinn Uile*' – 'We Are Brethren All'," I tell her as the audience of men, women and children around me listen so keenly to the lilting tune. "Father says it's about folk all being the same and how better the world should be if we considered ourselves family to one another."

And then I see Father look at Lachlan and nod over at me, and – in that strange and wonderful moment – I know what he wishes me to do.

Before I allow myself to feel nervous, I step forward to join my father and brother. Reaching a pause in the song, Lachlan turns to me and I begin translating the first verse into English as best I can.

"A happy home,
This old world would be,
If men while they're here,
Would try to agree.
And one could say to his neighbour
In cottage or hall,
'Come give me your hand,
We are family all...'"

I stop at that for I have not much of a voice. But even if I cannot sing sweet as a songbird, it does not much matter to the folk listening in the crowd, who seem to like the words very well and applaud for me, some of them brushing a tear away at the sentiment.

But I myself am so *very* far from tears. A hopeful smile slowly spreads across my sunburnt face as my gaze settles again on the rippling prairie, visible in the gaps between wooden buildings. For the farm we will settle on, it is somewhere out there, waiting for us, is it not?

A war ended, a blue sky, a fine family of sorts

and normal life.

Dare I think I might have found myself nearly home at last?

CHAPTER 15

Perhaps I am a strange creature, but though my twisted foot now aches so very badly, I am determined to walk this last stretch to our new home.

"Are you all right, Bridie?" asks Dr Spicer from the sitting board of the wagon, reins in hand. "Do you want to ride up here with me and Miss Kitty?"

"No, I'm fine," I lie as the fence comes into view, the fence Mr Campbell told us of in his directions to his homestead. *Our* soon-to-be homestead, which Father purchased from the Campbells since – as Easter guessed – the small-town life and their busy draper's store suits Mr and Mrs Campbell better than farming.

So what are the sights we have seen since we left Hopetoun, full as it was today with high hopes and high jinks?

A gushing, tripping river to the left of the rough track we travel along, with clusters of swaying bulrushes bristling at its edges.

To the other side of us, meadows that stretch on and

on, filled with flowers I do not yet know the names of, and no doubt some creatures I might be wary of getting acquainted with. (Sultan near enough reared *backwards* into the wagon when a snake slithered across our path not long ago.)

We watched as a pair of curious birds of prey spiralled above us, keeping their beady eyes on us – or more likely on the lookout for their dinner in the long grasses.

We came across a fierce, little white-faced possum that Patch took to chasing, till it chased her right back.

Then there was the farm we passed by, a hunched older man so lost in the business of his ploughing he did not hear Father helloing.

And now we are at a split in the track we have been travelling on – the left path leading towards the steep-sided riverbank, the right to the meadows and a not-too-distant low hill.

"We can't be far now," Father announces. "About half a mile more I think, perhaps a little less."

"Look! Mr Campbell told us to aim for that!" Lachlan says excitedly, pointing off towards the hillock I have already noticed.

"Clarice's Hill," Easter murmurs. She can't get over the romance of Mr Campbell naming it for his wife. Though I'm sure it had a name long before the couple bought the nearby homestead last year. The Ojibwe tribes of Minnesota – close relations of the Chippewas of Michigan – no doubt have a fine enough name for it that we might never know of.

But my thoughts suddenly drift as much as the lazy, hazy trail I now see. Puffs of smoke come directly from a tin chimney, a chimney that pokes *straight* out of the grass of the riverbank!

"Hey, that must be the dugout Mrs Campbell told us to look out for," I say, alerting everyone to the peculiar sight – a clue that directly below, unseen from the track, lies an earthen cave carved from the riverbank itself. It's currently home to some Irish family who are resting there before heading further west, Mrs Campbell said. Many riverside homesteaders have made shelters like this, Father has heard, as temporary living quarters till they build themselves proper wooden houses.

"Urgh!" squeals Miss Kitty, as if she has sniffed something more unpleasant than her mud-caked and sweat-stained clothes, perhaps. "I should *hate* to live in one of those. Like moles in a burrow!"

"They're no doubt fine people and we'll be sure to make their acquaintance another day," Father says more sensibly, before clicking his tongue to his teeth and urging the horses down the right-hand fork.

And soon enough, our tired feet and rumbling wagon follow where the wire-and-post fence leads us, which is to a wide wooden gate.

"'Campbell's Place'!" Easter calls out, running to

read the small, neatly painted sign tacked to it.

Father pulls Sultan and Queenie to a stop and Miss Kitty totters over – her once high-heeled boots worn down unevenly – to unhook the rope from the gate and let us pass through. From the front, Miss Kitty's blonde hair hangs in long, limp strands. But from where I stand, with her battered bonnet bobbing down her back by its faded ribbons, I can clearly see the spiky short hair where it grows again after being burned clean away the night of the party in her old house.

But I am quite used to the odd sight of Miss Kitty's mismatched hair by now. What I am *not* used to is this new view; the land within the fenced claim appears part wild as well as part farmed.

"Now, *this*," says Father, his voice rich with contentment, "will suit us very well I think."

"Yes," Dr Spicer agrees, and I watch as she closes her eyes and takes a deep breath of the very air her own child will draw in a couple of months time.

My younger brother is too excited to lumber alongside the slow-moving party that the rest of us are. With the gate open, Lachlan urges Pip into a trot and the two of them hurry on towards the small, squat house and stable we can just make out.

"It's not fair – if he gets there first, he's sure to take the best room for himself!" Miss Kitty cries out as she watches him go.

"Oh, I do not think that he will," I say, looking over at Easter and giving her a wink.

Easter knows as well as I do that the house is hardly likely to have much to it. Like all homesteaders, Mr and Mrs Campbell will not have had the funds or the time to build more than one or perhaps two rooms when they first settled on their claim.

"Shall we see?" says Easter, holding one hand out to me and the other to Miss Kitty.

And in a raggle-taggle line we girls run till we are quite caught up with my brother. He is – rather strangely – running his hand over the outside wall of our new home.

We slow to a stop, surveying what is in front of us.

"Well, if *that* is a house, then *I* am a chicken!" says Easter with a startled laugh.

"It's *earth*! Blocks of earth!" Lachlan shouts out in surprise, his fingers rubbing at the dry, crumbly, brown surface of the brick-like outside walls as Pip helps herself to the sweet high grasses that surround the place.

The wagon grinds to a halt beside us, and Sultan and Queenie's bursts of breath are like the sound of everyone's confusion.

"So it is a *sod* house?" Father laughs, as well he might, being a fine stonemason by trade. "Well, I have heard of soddies but never seen one. Let's take a closer look."

"Is it … is it *actually* built in 'bricks' made of earth?" I ask him, smiling yet dumbfounded.

"Cheapest material going," Father tells me. "No timber to cut and shape, no stone to cut to size. A fellow just slices rectangles straight out of the ground."

Lachlan has already pushed open the stiff, ungiving low door, shouting at us to follow him, and we do. The space inside, it is smaller than I expected – one room only with no furniture – but light and homely with a plaster that has been smoothed over the walls and ceiling and limewashed white.

"The stove I bought will sit there, by the chimney post," says Father. "And I'll quickly make us a table and stools since the Campbells took their furniture to town with them at the beginning of last winter."

I frown a little at the floor, wondering how we will fit in all our mattresses and bedding.

"The house will be for you ladies, of course," says Father, answering that question for me. "Lachlan and I will sleep in the wagon till such a time as I can cart lumber here and build us a bigger home."

In that instant I think of a certain "house" that makes this one seem quite the palace.

"Still, a sod house *has* to be better than a dugout!" I announce, which has one and all nodding and agreeing very quickly.

"Well, speaking of homes, today our president must

rightly be celebrating in his fine house in the capital," says Father gazing around at the four walls that are ours, all ours. "But I tell you, if Abraham Lincoln himself came here to visit, he would find no happier man than me..."

At that we all cheer, with the yaps of the pup Patch as accompaniment.

And with that happy sound, we are quite settled here in the Campbell's place.

Though as soon as Father next goes to town, I will ask him to bring back paint as I need to remake that sign by the gate, don't I? Because the MacKerries (and friends!) are here to stay...

CHAPTER 16

Of course, Abraham Lincoln will never visit our humble home.

And I truly mean never.

A peddler stopped by the farm yesterday and – as we inspected his pots and pans, candles and cutlery – told us the truly shocking news that President Lincoln had been shot dead, assassinated by a man whose loyalties lay with the Confederates. Tragically, it happened less than two weeks after the war ended.

"The sky is such a peculiar colour today, don't you think, girls?" Dr Spicer says to myself and Easter as she stands in the doorway of the sod house.

She looks from us, as we work in the small vegetable garden, to the receding wagon in the distance. The driver and passengers of the wagon are Father, Lachlan and Miss Kitty, who are trundling away along the track to town. They are already too far away for us to hear the clatter of Sultan and Queenie's hooves or the excited yelps of the pup in the bed of the wagon with my brother.

"It looks as if even the weather is in mourning for the president," I reply, glancing up at the strange grey-green pall of it.

"Well, I am so sorry, but I have no energy for the vegetable patch today," says Dr Spicer, resting her hands on her lower back. "If it's all right with you two young ladies, I might sit inside and read a while."

"Of course!" says Easter, standing up straight with a great handful of weeds clutched in her fist. "Get your rest while you can, before things get busy for you!"

Despite the awful news, Easter sounds as wise and sensible as she always does. "Mr Lincoln would not want us to stop and mourn him when we should still be celebrating the end of the war he helped bring about!" she said today. She's truly a credit to the pastor and his wife who brought her up.

As for myself, I still feel very raw and low after hearing of the tragedy. The others are distracting themselves by taking off to town; Father to sign the papers at the Land Office to make the homestead legally ours, Miss Kitty to buy soft cloth from the Campbells' store to make some things for the soon-to-come baby, and Lachlan to see if he can spot any other lads about his age, I think. He'd hoped to ride there on Pip, but the pony, like me, is a little lame after the weeks and miles of travelling we did.

"You know, you two girls should take some time to yourselves – why don't you go for a stroll?" says Dr Spicer, pausing before she goes inside. "We've all been so busy putting the place to rights that there's been no time to explore. Maybe you could go as far as one of our neighbours and say hello?"

"I'm not sure I am much in the mood to make polite conversation today," I say with a shrug. "But maybe a walk up the hill would be pleasant…"

"Yes, let's!" says Easter, throwing her fistful of weeds at the pile of kindling we'll later burn them on. "We'll surely see a view of our neighbours' places from up there, Dr Spicer, and can come and describe them to you!"

From up on high there'll be traces of the dugout visible, I suppose; a glint of the tin chimney and a haze of stove smoke. Another neighbour to the south of us is the older man Father called out to in his field. He is apparently married to an Ojibwe woman, who I am curious to meet (I'll practise the words Jean taught me; "*boozhoo*" for a greeting, "*aaniish ndishnikaaz Bridie*" to introduce myself). On the far side of the hill we have heard that two sisters have a homestead. How my heart raced when I first knew, imagining – just for a foolish moment – that some shining, invisible thread had brought my missing sisters close again! But I very quickly – and disappointingly – found out that the sisters are in their thirties and come from Boston.

After a glance at the curious sky, I pull my shawl around me and am about to set off with Easter when an odd, strangled whinny from Pip stops us both in our tracks. With a quick, questioning glance toward my friend, I go to where Pip is tethered to a post close by, her hooves stomping in the rough grass.

"Hello, there," I say, nuzzling Pip's warm, soft nose in my hand. "Are you restless too? Don't worry; you'll soon enough be busy taking the doctor to visit her new patients about the county!"

There's a dainty, two-wheeled gig ready and waiting for that day, left here by the Campbells and for which Dr Spicer has paid them. After months left in out in poor weather it's in need of some repair, but it'll be a pretty thing when it's fixed up. Yellow, Dr Spicer wants it painted. And Lachlan has already got Pip used to the feel of pulling it, walking her gently around the claim.

"What's wrong?" I ask, as Pip's ears twitch frantically. She backs away, eyes white and rolling.

And then I hear it – the silence.

A few minutes ago, I now realise, the air was full of the songs and chirrups of birds and insects. And now; now there is nothing.

I look around hoping I see something, *anything* to explain the eerie quiet.

"What is it?" I hear Easter ask, her voice tight.

"I don't know…" I mutter in response, looking around and above me.

If I was on Tornish, I'd perhaps expect to see a tumult of bruised black storm clouds rushing in on a gathering wind. But there are no fat, bulging storm clouds, and there *is* no wind; there is not the slightest stirring of air. All there is is the queer grey-green tinge to the hunkering sky and no sounds at all.

Except for a faint whine.

I turn my head this way and that, trying to place where it comes from … and I see that Easter is doing the same.

"Girls?" comes a thin, slightly strangled call. "Bridie… Easter… Oh dear God, I think the baby is coming … and it is much too early!"

At that moment my head should be turned towards the tiny sod house and the drama that is unfolding within it.

But the trouble is, something *else* is coming.

A great grey wall it is, rising thick and eerie from behind Clarice's Hill…

"Please, please, *please*," I utter over and over as I flick the reins, urging Pip on along the track from our little farm.

I am begging for so very many things in this moment.

I am begging Pip's sore leg to stand the running

I am asking her to do.

I am begging the swaying, bucking, wooden gig to hold together.

I am begging the strange wall of the storm to roll away east, to leave us and the town alone. I have never seen the like of it in my life – a great grey wave rising *miles* in the sky. If I were not so frightened by it, I'd laugh at myself for wondering what the flowers of this region were called when I'd have better spent my time learning the treacherous ways of its weather.

And lastly and most importantly, I am begging whoever in the universe will listen that Easter can help the barely conscious Dr Spicer and her unborn babe stay alive till I get help.

"Please!" I cry out, feeling the still air pick up into a spritely, slapping breeze at last, which I can't help but think is *not* a good sign.

But all I need to do is catch up with the wagon so that I might direct Father to urgently seek out the midwife in town whom Mrs Campbell told us of, and very quickly return with her.

And I *should* be able to see Father and the others soon; I lost time struggling to back a reluctant Pip into the shafts of the gig, as well as trying to remember which parts of leather straps and collars and traces needed to be fixed where and how. But we two are dashing at some speed now and surely the wagon would not go particularly fast, what with three folk loading it down…

But as I race towards the fork in the road where I'll join the riverside track, the gig lurches unnervingly on one side with every rotation and I have to pull Pip up, terrified that one of the wheels will come off altogether. What use would I be to Dr Spicer if *I'm* lying broken in the road beside it?

Panic – as well as wind-tangled hair – makes me blind for a moment, till I feel Pip come to a nervous, panting stop, and I push my hair from my face with a shaking hand.

And then I see my salvation, and Dr Spicer and her baby's possible best hope – those puffs of grey smoke undulating from the tin chimney in the ground. We are close to the dugout and, more importantly, someone appears to be home.

Jumping from the gig, I grab Pip by the halter and hurry towards the river. A rough sort of lane appears to lead down towards a wide, flat patch of rough grass and stone, with the river on one side and the tall earthen bank – with the strange house built directly into it – on the other. I don't know if I dare force Pip and the gig down there, but then again, I daren't leave her up here with nothing to tie her to; she is so frightened and skittish she'd run off I fear.

So I do the only thing I can; I tilt my head back and roar.

"HELP! HELP ME, PLEASE! HELP!" I plead at the top of my screeching, desperate voice, hoping one of the Irish family can hear me, tucked away as they are in their burrow home.

Using every ounce of strength to shout, I don't clearly hear the door being dragged open or the first words the concerned-looking woman calls out.

But as I see her pick up her skirts and run up to me, I gasp and gulp myself quiet and try to settle on the words she is saying to me.

"What are you doing out when there's a tornado coming, lassie?" she bellows, her eyes full of kindness and alarm. "Come down here at once, *a thasgaid*! And why is there blood all over your face?"

She called me "lassie".

She called me "dear" in Gaelic.

So it seems Mrs Campbell got it wrong – as many do – muddling the sound of an Irish voice and a Scots voice. And as the woman from the dugout understands and uses Gaelic, it means she is most likely from the Highlands and Islands of Scotland...

And so the Highland Scots woman is up to me now, her hand on my cheek, and I realise the blood she speaks of comes from the cut on my hand where I must have caught my fingers in the rush to harness Pip back in the soddie stable.

This woman's face, now close to me ... how strange

it is, but I'd swear on my mother's grave that it is *so* familiar. If my rattled mind would stay still enough to let me place it, I would surely remember who—

Suddenly I tremble with shock, with relief, with streaming tears when I see who runs up from the dugout to help. Everything now fits into place.

"Little Bird? Little Bird!" my dear, darling friend from Tornish calls out to me.

Will is here.

Here, like a miracle from the past to help me in the present.

CHAPTER 17

Four years we've been apart, Will and I, with stories to tell each other that span thousands of miles and half a world.

But all we have time for is a hug that cannot last and a few hurried exchanges; the gathering wind seems to buffet and suck us away from each other, as well as the words from our very mouths.

"How can this be? What in heaven's name brings you to our door, Bridie MacKerrie?" asks Will's mother, putting her warm hands on my wet cheeks as if she needs to prove I am a living, breathing girl and no trick of her imagination.

Where and how do I begin? I have not a single moment to spare to tell her of our two years in Glasgow after we fled the island, of our time in New York.

"We've recently come from Michigan – we've bought the Campbells' place over the way, Mistress Beaton," I say, politely addressing the dear lady the way I always did back in Scotland. But even as I reply to her, my eyes are quickly trying to drink in the sight of Will.

He is quite different from the boy I once knew; he now towers over me, all gawky limbs, grown tall as my father, if not taller. But in his familiar brush of fair hair and that gap-toothed grin I see my treasured twelve-year-old friend, my boy from Tornish.

"Are your father and Lachlan at the Campbells' homestead now?" Will asks as he grabs Pip by the head collar to hold her as steady as he can.

"They're gone to town," I say, hoping all are safe at the Campbells' store, with Sultan and Queenie unhitched from the wagon and inside some stable or shelter. "But we have a lady in trouble at the house — she is having a baby. It's coming too early and she is in a great deal of pain. My friend Easter is with her but things aren't right."

"Oh, that poor woman!" mumbles Mistress Beaton, her mind running with outcomes — good and bad — I can tell.

"My father's in town too, so we don't have the wagon," Will says partly to me, partly to his mother.

"Do you think the wee cart can take the two of us, Bridie?" Mistress Beaton asks me as she looks dubiously upon the flimsy gig.

"We can try," I say, since it is the difference between a few minutes' ride and a twenty-minute walk to the soddie.

And sure enough, a very short time later – with creaks and cracks that I felt sure might send the gig splintering from under us – Mistress Beaton and I find ourselves outside the sod-built farmhouse.

"Dr Spicer! I'm here!" I call out, though with the wind's walloping strength I'm being blown back and forward and sideways as I try to dismount and keep hold of Pip, and so no words, I think, will reach the struggling lady and Easter inside.

"Hello!" I hear Will's mother boom in her loud, friendly voice as she jumps down from the gig and bursts straight in through the door with no pause. "My name's Agnes Beaton, ma'am, and I'm here to help..."

I'll surely get myself inside to help too, just as soon as I can get Pip unhitched and into the earthen-brick stable next to the low-slung house. But again, the forceful, jousting wind is out to confound and confuse me, playing with me like a cat plays with a half-dead mouse. The cut on my hand opens and bleeds again as I struggle to keep my balance and unfasten the thick leather straps and buckles and set the pony free from the now rocking, tilting gig that threatens to tip clean over.

"Here!" yells a voice in my ear. "Hold this!"

And I find that I have the reins of a grey-muzzled mule pushed into my hand, and that *I* myself am being pushed to the side by Will.

But I am grateful for his actions and his energy, and

while he takes over my wrestlings with the trappings of the cart, I grab both Pip and the mule by their head harnesses and hold tight, though the tossing of their strong necks near wrenches my wrists from my arms.

"Go!" Will shouts just as I worry that my weak hand can't keep a grip of Pip half a moment longer.

We both run the animals to the stable, where I pull aside the wooden door of it and we haul them into the gloom. I tie Pip to a post by one wall, while Will looks around, spies a post by the opposite wall, and fastens his mule to it. At least they are far enough away not to kick each other in their panic. And now we must get out before the foam-mouthed creatures kick *us*.

As I fasten the door tight shut on them, I turn and finally take a proper look at what terrible mischief is happening in the sky.

The bank of dark grey that rises up from the horizon – it has a blacker shape forming inside it now.

"It's a tornado!" Will shouts in my ear, holding me tight by the arm. "It's going to touch down!"

As the moving, shifting funnel fixes on the ground in the all-too-near distance, I feel the rushing swoop of air still for just a second.

A second where I can clearly hear a baby's frail cry of life in the midst of the storm's madness...

CHAPTER 18

The sounds in the busy dining room are of cutlery chinking against plates, of polite chatter – and Will's storytelling.

"That was the very *minute* you were born, Franny, when the tornado came down, down, *down* and the tip of it *crashed* into the ground," says Will, bouncing the baby on his knee in time with each dramatic word.

Franny, tiny scrap that she is, named after the father she'll never know, has her blue eyes wide and fixed on Will's face. We are all of us quite mad for her, but perhaps I the most. Is she not another girl born too soon, in a storm, just as *I* was?

And like me, here she is, hale and hearty. She is exactly eleven weeks old and on her first adventure, taking a trip to the bustling town of St Paul. My little Sugar Moon I call her, for being born in the month of April.

Easter – savouring the last of her sugared honey biscuit – pulls a face at me, amused and charmed by

Will's devotion to Dr Spicer's child.

"Lucky for you the winds turned and the tornado headed away east from us," Will carries on, "or a wee thing like you might have been taken up, up, *up* into the twister, like *this*! Whee!"

Will lifts the baby clear up into the air.

"Hey!" Easter calls out.

"Don't frighten her, Will!" I add to my friend's protective warning.

"*Ist*, Little Bird! She loves it!" He laughs as Franny gurgles and wriggles.

"What makes you so sure about that, Will Beaton?" I ask him, pushing aside the empty plate in front of me now that I have finished my own biscuit.

"Well, look how she's smiling," he says, clearly delighted.

"She's not smiling – she's pulling a face," Easter points out.

"Yes, the poor child's probably troubled with wind," I add.

"Och, you're just jealous, Bridie," Will says lightly to me. "Franny obviously likes *me* more than she likes either of you two."

"You think *we're* jealous of *you*?" I say, pretending to choke at the very idea, while Easter throws her head back and laughs. "That's like saying a fine horse such as Sultan is jealous of a dirt-grubbing gopher!"

I cannot say how fond I am of this merry bickering and teasing. Oh, how I have missed it!

"*Don't* you listen to them, Franny!" Will orders the rosebud-lipped babe, who stares at him hard as he lowers her back down.

Others are staring too. Fellow customers here in the dining room look upon Will with differing opinions, I think; the ladies smiling with melting hearts to see a young lad so caring to one so small, while several of the men scowl, as if Will is a fool to do a woman's work when two girls sit right by him.

"You know, Little Bird has *never* been kind to me, Franny," he jokes, jiggling the cooing child. "There was a time when I waved and *waved* to her from the top of a hill on an island, but she kept on sailing away..."

I freeze at those words of his. The memory of escaping from Tornish and having to leave Will and so many folk behind to an unknown future still cuts me deep.

"And it was the same *again* when she set off from Glasgow," he cheerfully continues. "Can you believe she didn't have the ship stopped and turned right around?"

Yes, he has already confirmed it; when the *Ailsa Craig* took its leave from Scotland with Father, Lachlan and myself onboard, I did *not* imagine that I saw Will waving at me... He *was* standing by my sister Effie on the flatbed cart, his arms windmilling in my direction. His family were newly arrived in Glasgow and had been at the Anchor Line ticket office trying to decide what their overseas destination should be.

And I can only give thanks that we did not miss each other *here* in Minnesota, though that was a close call. I am so very happy that Will's parents have changed their minds about setting off further west now they know my family is settled in the district of Hopetoun. In fact Mr Beaton is at this moment toiling alongside Father, Lachlan and the neighbouring farmer, all helping build our new lumber house.

It is painfully disappointing, however, to find out that Will has no news of what became of Ishbel and Effie. In the confusion of the crowds at the harbour, he was quickly parted from my sister and the rest of our farewell party…

As Dr Spicer often says, it may be hoped that modern wonders like electricity and better medicine will improve and save the lives of folk in the future. I just hope too that there will come a day when someone invents a means by which loved ones will *never* be lost to one another, no matter where in the world they may be…

"And Little Bird didn't even want me to come with you all today!" I hear Will prattle on to the baby.

Easter smirks my way when she hears that fake

self-pitying comment.

"Look, it's not that I didn't *want* you to come with us, Will – we're glad of your company. We just didn't *need* you to come," I try to explain. "It's Father I'm cross with, not you. Dr Spicer and Easter and I hardly required an escort to 'protect' us!"

"Aw, it's just because he cares about you so much," Will replies, turning his face to me. His grin is cheeky and his raised eyebrows are knowing.

"Stop that!" I tell him off.

Will just grins all the wider. I understand his meaning quite clearly; he is certain that Father is smitten with Dr Spicer and will have none of it when I tell him again and again that they are just friends, as he and I are.

Oh, but I'd forgotten how infuriating he could be!

"Right, that's done. Our bill is paid," I hear Dr Spicer suddenly announce as she strides over to us, picking up the cradleboard from where she leant it against the wall.

Putting her arms through the two leather straps of it, the doctor expertly hoists the birchbark board up on to her shoulders and back, and waits while Easter whisks the baby from Will and carefully slots her into the beadwork embroidered bag that is fastened to it. I quickly help tuck Franny into her cosy cocoon lined with the softest rabbit fur – Jean's gift to Dr Spicer before we all left Hawk's Point.

"Let's go!" Dr Spicer announces, completely blind

to – or unbothered by – the renewed stares of the other customers, who have probably never seen a respectable white woman stride about St Paul with a baby in a Chippewa cradleboard.

All their jaws appear to hang open, as if a shoal of herring watches us make our way out of the tinkling-belled door.

"So, the instructions say that the mansion house is in *this* direction," says Dr Spicer, weaving in and out of the folk that mill this way and that, some calm and clear-eyed locals, some new arrivals that must have just stepped or stumbled off one of the many magnificent riverboats moored here after churning their enormous circular paddles up the wide Mississippi river. These newcomers gawp at the noise and chaos of the new town that is being frantically built about them, just as *we* have done since we disembarked from the stagecoach that brought us here earlier.

Who knows what has brought so many new arrivals to St Paul, what hopes and dreams they might have. But I know *our* reason; it so happens that the phenomenally rich gentleman who *owns* most of the riverboats – as well as the Minnesota Stage Company – is one Mr James C. Burbank. I have only very recently found out about his existence, not being previously aware of him in our particular corner of the state.

I have also found out that Mr James C. Burbank is

not satisfied with simply being rich and well-respected; he also wants to show the good people of the territory that he is an extremely cultured man. He wants to be admired for his taste, not just in the mansion he has had built and furnished overlooking the town, but by showing his interest and patronage of the arts. And as a man of the modern age, he has chosen to show an exhibition of a revolutionary style of photography at his house this afternoon. Attending this exhibition will be state dignitaries, fellow business magnates, plenty of other fancy folk I suppose – and me.

"You have your invitation, Bridie?" Dr Spicer checks after we have gradually wended our way uphill for some time, passing grander and grander houses and gardens at every turn.

"I do," I reply, patting my skirt pocket as we finally find ourselves looking across vast lawns and trees to a house on its own at the crest of the hill.

I can scarcely believe that I have been included in this gathering at all, but I have the gilt-edged, thick-papered invitation to prove it, along with the explanatory letter Jakob Wahle sent with it. The letter was addressed simply to: "Little Bird, care of the Post Office, Hopetoun, Minnesota". It got to me with little trouble. (If only ALL letters could find their recipients so easily, wouldn't that be a fine thing?) It read:

LITTLE BIRD LANDS

Mr James C. Burbank is kindly displaying many of my 'Combination Printing' portraits and landscapes.

Your portrait is his particular favourite, and when he found out you live just a half-day's journey north by stagecoach, he was quite determined that you come, as guest of honour!

To be guest of honour – truthfully, it fills me with as much dread as it does excitement, considering the events that unfolded after the *last* time I was singled out for such special treatment back at the mine manager's house in Hawk's Point.

"Is that it?" asks Easter, pointing to the remarkable-looking, three-storey house, one that would sit very well in the most fashionable neighbourhoods of New York or Glasgow. It is quite awash with arched windows and ornamental turrets and what seems like an excessive amount of porches.

"I should think it is," says Dr Spicer with a nod.

"I bet Miss Kitty would've liked to see such a fancy place as this!" Will adds, as we start up the long drive to the big house.

"I bet she would not care for it at all," I reply, remembering that Will has not quite forgotten (or forgiven) the spoilt, rich girl that she once was.

But the truth is, Miss Kitty has no interest in going anywhere but Hopetoun these days. She is happy at the farm, and happy working at Mrs Campbell's drapery store, where she impresses the customers with her pert English accent.

"So, are you ready, Bridie?" Dr Spicer turns and asks me as we see some suited gentlemen ahead of us being greeted at the front door, just as their glossy carriage and prancing horses are driven away by a liveried driver.

"No," I reply, feeling my heart start to race.

"Well, take a deep breath and remember—"

"There is nothing that can stop me doing whatever I set my mind to!" I finish for her, hoping my heart doesn't burst out of my chest as, with a shaking hand, I hold out my invitation to the gentlemanly servant at the door (a butler, or footman, perhaps?)

I am in a little of an agitated state as we are ushered inside the mansion. The buzzing chatter of the milling crowd in the large room we are shown into feels almost as if there is a fog of *bees* about me, and I struggle to take in the beautifully dressed men and women, the mirror-panelled walls, the layered chandeliers, the many framed photographs displayed on their tall wooden stands.

"Little Bird! You are here!"

Suddenly my good hand is lifted – and kissed, would you believe?

"Mr Wahle! I— We— Hello!" I say in a stumbling fashion.

"I am so pleased you could come," says the

photographer, looking very smart in a chocolate-coloured suit and waistcoat.

He appears both delighted and quite beside himself, as he should do. From a hard-working but undoubtedly poorly paid travelling tintype salesman, he has elevated himself to something quite splendid. An artist, no less.

"Hello, Mr Wahle. I'm Dr Stephanie Spicer, friend of Bridie's – Little Bird's – family," says the doctor, introducing herself since I seem to be unable to. "And this is Easter and Will, *also* friends of the family…"

"Ah, yes! I recall seeing you in Hopetoun, Miss Easter, on the day that peace was declared," says the photographer, making my friend smile in surprise as she finds her *own* hand kissed.

Then he turns his attention to the youngest of our group.

"And this little one?" Mr Wahle laughs as he plays peekaboo at Franny in her cradleboard.

"My daughter," the doctor explains. "Now which gentleman is Mr Burbank?"

Dr Spicer's eyes are bright; I know that offering to accompany me here today was a kindness to Father who was too busy back at the farm to come away. But Dr Spicer has reasons of her own for wanting to meet Mr James C. Burbank. He and other wealthy gentlemen of the city are talking of the possibility of a university being built in St Paul. She would like to converse with him about whether that will include a medical school I think. One that will be happy to train women I have no doubt, and might require an experienced female physician to teach them!

"I am not sure where exactly Mr Burbank is at the moment," Mr Wahle replies, looking round at the crowds. "But for now, let me show you your portrait, Little Bird! I have just been told that there is a group here *very* taken with it. They are newly arrived from Italy! Come…"

And so I find myself drawn forward, the sea of people parting as Mr Wahle ushers us towards the largest of the photographic portraits, set on an easel in the middle of the vast and bustling room.

"Look at you, Bridie!" I am vaguely aware of Easter saying with her usual joyful laugh of surprise.

Equally, I am only vaguely aware of the fancily dressed folk – the Italian group Mr Wahle mentioned – that stand closest to the framed portrait. The two women and the man who holds a baby in his arms turn as I come closer, and kindly step aside to let me see myself.

And there I am; or a version of me. A girl lost in thoughts and dreamings, set against a backdrop of prairie grass and Minnesota skies. But the sight of it is so strangely, wonderfully familiar. For Mr Wahle's photographic image is *so* very like the sketch that

LITTLE BIRD LANDS

Samuel Mitford once drew of me long ago and far away in Scotland…

"Little Bird!" Will's urgent voice catches my attention.

Before I can ask him what the matter is, I feel a gentle hand rest upon my arm. Turning, I see that one of the ladies of the Italian party is gazing intently at me, her light-coloured eyes pooling with tears.

The elegantly dressed young woman is like a painting herself, her high cheek-boned face and neat black hair visible below her daintily perched hat with its cascade of ribbons and silk flowers.

But then my heart nearly stops as I stare at her, as her face becomes known to me. For – rather than a painting – didn't Father *always* compare my striking eldest sister to some statue of a Greek goddess from antiquity.

"Oh, Bridie… Bridie!" Ishbel whispers my name as if she has seen a spirit.

"Are you truly real? How can this be?" another voice adds, laughing, sobbing. Effie. It is Effie!

But I am no spirit, no ghost, no will-o'-the-wisp.

Shock may have temporarily stolen my words away, but I quickly throw my arms around both my sisters so they can know I am flesh and I am blood and I am *theirs* now and always…

CHAPTER 19

Once upon a time, in a wee box bed in a snug stone house, three young sisters slept.

Though in truth only the elder two girls slept soundly, tossing in their nightly meanderings, blissfully unaware of the sharp elbows and knees they inflicted on the littlest sister, who herself slept – fitfully – between them.

My, how far we three have come from those quiet days on our small Scottish island where we expected to live our whole lives! And now I can barely believe my luck, that I have Ishbel and Effie standing beside me in the warm June sunshine, here on Clarice's Hill in Minnesota.

What twists and turns we have all taken to get here! My lost letters never reached either of my sisters because fate took them far from where they expected to be. Effie left Glasgow after her mistress's death and went to join Ishbel ... but not in London. Samuel's work there fell through and instead he took another commission in Italy. The pleasant party of Effie, Ishbel, Samuel and

Caroline — along with Patch the old terrier — set off for Europe.

Happily, their number swelled by one the day Caroline gave birth to a daughter. Sadly, it *sank* by one the very same day when Caroline slipped out of this world…

"You're right, Bridie, it's a grand outlook," says Ishbel now, with one hand shading her eyes as she takes in the view, and the other hugging me tight at my waist.

My sisters, Samuel and baby Florence — named for the Italian city she was born in — are visiting us from St Paul where they are very settled. The new towns and cities of the west are full of up-and-coming businessmen who wish to have their portraits painted and hung in their offices and boardrooms.

"You know, Ishbel and I were *so* happy to come to America after Italy," says Effie, who herself stands like a mirror image to Ishbel, her arm slipped similarly around me. Her wavy hair is buffeted in the wind atop Clarice's Hill and a few loose, red tendrils of it tickle my cheek. "We both felt that we would be somehow closer to you and Father and Lachlan wherever you were."

"Though it did seem so very foolish to hope that we might ever find you all," adds Ishbel with her usual tone of caution.

"Yet you did!" I laugh as I think of the waves of people from their old countries, leaving all those whisper trails and invisible threads for the people who come next, making this vast land just that little bit smaller.

"Wait … hear that? Father's playing his whistle!" says Effie, pointing down towards the newly finished two-storey lumber house and the tiny figures of folk milling around out front preparing for our celebration. "What tune *is* that?"

We all pause, trying to catch the lilt. The old dog that followed us up here and promptly fell asleep – even *he* raises a tired head at the sweet sound of it.

"Is it not your favourite, Effie, 'The Fairy Love Song'?" I suggest, remembering the last time I heard it when I woke from my fever in the parlour of the store in Hawk's Point. "'If I saw you coming, I would run to meet you…'"

It suddenly makes me think of Jean Paquette and I wonder if we will ever see him again. But if I have learned anything these last few days, it is that there is always, *always* a chance. I know that Father has already written to Mrs Drummond, telling her that if the roads of New York City have crept too close to her farmyard for comfort, we would warmly welcome her, Marthy-Jane and the little girl's home-from-the-war father as neighbours here in Hopetoun County.

"Oh, my goodness … is that my Samuel dancing, with a *baby* in each arm?" says Ishbel, scrunching her eyes the better to see the folk below.

LITTLE BIRD LANDS

Our Franny and little Florence have delighted in each other since they first met the day of the exhibition in Mr Burbank's mansion. They are like cousins, though they are not truly kin. But then when have *I* ever worried about what kin means exactly? Easter and even Miss Kitty have become as much sisters to me as Effie and Ishbel, Dr Spicer like an aunt, or even – dare I say it – much more…

"Is that safe?" Ishbel frets. "What if he drops them!"

"I'm sure they will be fine," I tell her, seeing Easter dance close, ready – as ever – to lend a hand if she needs to.

But Samuel seems like a doting and careful father. And from what I have seen, Ishbel is a loving stepmother to Caroline's child. I am sure our old friend would be happy to know that as Samuel and Ishbel grieved her loss, they slowly felt a love grow between them and were recently married.

"I think we had better get back down," says Ishbel, clearly not convinced that doing a jig with babies is the best thing for the little girls, though I don't see Dr Spicer or Miss Kitty or any of the others rushing to their aid.

"And we'd better lend a hand – all your neighbours and friends will be arriving soon for the house-warming," Effie adds, setting off after Ishbel, the skirts of their dresses looking like a pair of pealing bells rocking from side to side as they skitter away down the rough path.

Indeed it looks as if our visitors are beginning to arrive already. I can see the Beatons' wagon just driving up and Lachlan and his ever-growing pup running to greet them. Our nearby farming neighbours, as well as Mr and Mrs Campbell, are expected too.

"What a day, eh, Patch?" I say to the elderly dog panting at my feet.

The scruffy, slightly lame cairn terrier who I never thought I would see again, looks up at me, one ear up, one ear down, as if he is listening attentively.

"What adventures we have had, you and I..." I murmur to him, thinking of the days he'd trot after Will and myself around the island, to the lochan, the standing stones, to the rocky top of the Glas Crags. And of course he has had his *own* adventures with my sisters these last few years, accompanying them to Europe and now America no less!

And what adventures are there to come, I wonder as I wave back to the windmilling figure of Will in the yard, who has spied me up here.

For a start, I will be teaching school in Hopetoun at the end of summer, though both Easter and I harbour a not-so-secret wish that one day we might follow in Dr Spicer's footsteps and train to be doctors, if a medical school ever opens in St Paul or Minneapolis. Easter does sometimes worry that being not just a female, but one with brown skin, might make that difficult, but I have reminded her that the Civil War has changed everything.

She sometimes looks a little doubtful when I say that, but I am certain the time is coming when Easter and I and *every* girl can do and be what they want if they set their minds to it.

And you never know, though I love it here in Hopetoun County, one day I might decide to travel *further* west to see where the next horizon takes me!

The smile that comes with that wonderful possibility fades a little as I suddenly think of the *one* person I will never meet again, no matter if I had all the luck in the world. I don't suppose I will ever travel back to Tornish, or visit the church graveyard, or place my hand on Mother's small and neat headstone. But then whenever I want I can be there! All I need to do is come up here to the top of Clarice's Hill, lift my head to the sky and imagine myself lifting, rising, soaring like a migrating bird flying from the warm winds of Minnesota to the brisk breezes of that small Scottish island, where I'll land by the fragrant purple heather of my old home.

In the meantime, this trusty old dog here is beginning to weary of my daydreaming when there is the smell of cooking drifting from the campfire and is whimpering his impatience.

235

"Come on, then," I say cheerfully and make to go.

Patch and I set off down the hill, both of us limping a little, certainly, but both as sure and steady as can be.

A NOTE FROM THE AUTHOR

Writing *Little Bird Lands* – and its partner book *Little Bird Flies* – has honestly been the most amazing experience of my writing life. Yes, I absolutely knew the story I wanted to weave, but I didn't realise I'd find myself so totally engrossed in a treasure trove of research as I mapped out Bridie's adventures.

Some of the details I uncovered for this novel were small and special, like the beautiful Ojibwe/Chippewa terms for the months of the year. Some were startling, like the attempted terrorist attacks in New York near the end of the Civil War. All have made me even more amazed at the experience of my Scottish forebears, poor farming families suddenly finding themselves thrust into an overwhelming new world, and discovering that "freedom" would be a long and winding road.

And of course, while I was telling the story through the eyes of a young, immigrant Scottish girl, I had the privilege of finding out more about the history of the particular Native Americans of the region I was writing about, as well as that of free black people in the northern states.

There was so much I learned about the Ojibwe/Chippewa people that I couldn't fit into this book. If you'd like to find out more, I really recommend *The Birchbark House* series of children's books by Louise Erdrich; they tell the story of an Ojibwe girl and her community in the mid 1800s. I was already a big fan of the *Little House* series by Laura Ingalls Wilder, which tell the tales of Laura and her white-settler family travelling in the west. Reading about children's experiences at that time on both sides – Native American and white homesteader – gave me real insight as well as food for thought. You might also like to look at this online classroom resource: www.bigorrin.org/chippewa_kids.htm.

By the way, nowadays, Native American is the most preferred, respectful term for the USA's indigenous people, but I used Indian in the novel as this would have been authentic for the nineteenth-century setting. I also describe Jean as Chippewa, rather than Ojibwe; it's a variation of the same name, but again, Chippewa was more commonly used by settlers in the Michigan region at that time.

Speaking of homesteaders, I was fascinated to read about black pioneers of the era. Of course the horrors of the slave trade in the American south quite rightly dominate our idea of black history in the eighteen hundreds, but after reading and discovering how many free black people in the north took the opportunity to head out in covered wagons and find farming land in the sprawling prairies of the west, I was inspired to include Mr and Mrs Campbell's journey as well as write about Easter's hopes for an independent future of her own.

It was a privilege to learn what I did along the way. I hope you enjoy the journey you've taken with Bridie, and – like her and like me – come to think about the difficulties and dreams of *everyone* who wants a place to call home.

ACKNOWLEDGEMENTS

This is the tucked away section of a book where people are thanked by an author for their hand holding, rah-rah-rah-ing and general, invaluable efforts to make it the best it can be. And I *will* come to the people who helped *Little Bird Lands* take flight, but first I'm going to start by thanking three *places* which have shaped my writing...

Authors are daydreamers, and my daydreaming started in Flat 87, Denburn Court, Aberdeen, Scotland. On the fifteenth floor of this high-rise tower block, I'd stare from my childhood bedroom window at the view of the North Sea, with oil rigs dotted on its steely grey surface. I'd stare at the city's streets below, teeming with local residents, but also with the Americans, French and Dutch who'd settled in my hometown due to the oil boom for which it had become famous. I daydreamed about other people's lives and stories, and what lay beyond the sea and the horizon. And when I tired of staring out of the window, I flopped on my bed and lost myself in the world of books.

Cue the *next* place I'm thankful for... From my window up on high I also looked down on the impressive, granite-built Central Library. It was my wonderland. I'd borrow armfuls of fiction and those stories, those endless stories, were both a gateway and an escape for me. Finding myself transported from a modern bedroom to nineteenth-century America with Laura Ingalls Wilder's *Little House on the Prairie* series of books was a real game changer. Suddenly, history became accessible; I was walking side-by-side with children who lived in the past.

Bringing us up to the present, I've been an author for many years, writing my own books at a desk in a small room at the back of my terraced house. But staying at home day and night can make your brain stall, so I'm often to be found at my second office, the local garden-centre cafe, which is flooded with light, surrounded by plants and gives me the opportunity to pat the occasional passing dog. In the last few months, fellow customers will have had no idea that the person tippetty-tapping on a laptop in the corner was actually lost in nineteenth-century New York, Michigan and Minnesota...

And now for the real, live humans! Huge thanks go to the editorial team of Kirsty Stansfield, Fiona Scoble and Maurice Lyon for kindly comments and word-wrangling. I also bow down to art director Nicola Theobald for the delicious look of both *Little Bird Flies* and *Little Bird Lands*, and for finding the amazing Jasu Hu to illustrate the covers, as well as Hannah Horn for the incredibly detailed maps inside both books. I also want to give a shout-out to US author Caroline Starr Rose, whose novel-in-verse *May B* – the story of one gruelling winter in the life of a twelve-year-old pioneer's daughter – made me even more excited about writing my *own* pioneer story from an immigrant's point of view.

Finally, I just want to say I owe a huge debt to the authors of a zillion non-fiction books about experiences of life in eighteen-hundreds Scotland and America. The same goes for the writers of numerous websites and blogs. There are so, so many I could fill another book with my thanks to them all. With this background of research, I've done my very best to give an authentic snapshot of a period of history, seen through the eyes of Scottish émigré Bridie MacKerrie. I've tried immensely hard to make sure all the detail is correct, but I hold my hands up if I accidentally got anything wrong.

My hope is that readers will enjoy walking side by side with Little Bird, of course. But if this novel makes some readers want to explore further – to read about the Highland Clearances of Scotland, the melting-pot roots of modern-day USA, the Native Americans whose home the nation was first – then

I'll be very happy to know they were as curious and as fascinated as I have been on this transaltantic journey.

MORE GREAT FICTION
FROM NOSY CROW

"A gripping, moving piece of historical fiction."
– Imogen Russell Williams, *Guardian*

"A fast-paced adventure, whose elegant prose and
cliffhanger chapters should keep even less confident
readers gripped to the thrilling end."
– Emily Bearn, *Telegraph*

The Times Children's Book of the Week

Nominated for the CILIP Carnegie Medal

MORE GREAT FICTION
FROM NOSY CROW

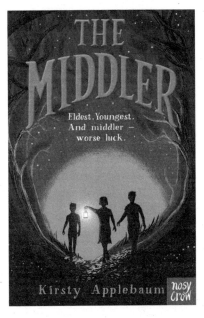

"This is a quirky, original adventure about friendship and loyalty, betrayal and trust, kindness and greed, told as Maggie's vibrant narrative, with striking characters and a happy ending in which all siblings are equal."
– Nicolette Jones, *The Sunday Times*

The Times Children's Book of the Week

The Sunday Times Children's Book of the Week

Nominated for the CILIP Carnegie Medal